Readers love
JOHN INMAN

Head-on

"This is an outstanding book. It will make you smile. It will make you cry. It will make you rethink a lot of things you may do every day."
—On Top Down Under Reviews

"*Head-on* was a love at first read for me and it just confirms why I always get territorial and do the "HANDS OFF IT'S MINE!" routine whenever a new John story comes up for release…"
—Sinfully Sexy Book Reviews

Paulie

"I absolutely adore what I've read from John Inman so far and *Paulie* is another winner for me."
—The Novel Approach

Spirit

"Besides it being well-written in a casual, but effective manner—with endearing main characters and malevolent villains—it's also touching and funny."
—Rainbow Book Reviews

"John's writing just draws you right in. It's never over the top, but instead the funny moments just fit right into the narrative and dialogue organically…"
—My Fiction Nook

By JOHN INMAN

A Hard Winter Rain
Head-on
Hobbled
Jasper's Mountain
Loving Hector
Paulie
Payback
The Poodle Apocalypse
Shy
Snow on the Roof (Dreamspinner Anthology)
Spirit

THE BELLADONNA ARMS
Serenading Stanley
Work in Progress

Published by DREAMSPINNER PRESS
http://www.dreamspinnerpress.com

Payback

JOHN INMAN

Dreamspinner Press

Published by
DREAMSPINNER PRESS

5032 Capital Circle SW, Suite 2, PMB# 279, Tallahassee, FL 32305-7886 USA
http://www.dreamspinnerpress.com/

This is a work of fiction. Names, characters, places, and incidents either are the product of author imagination or are used fictitiously, and any resemblance to actual persons, living or dead, business establishments, events, or locales is entirely coincidental.

Payback
© 2015 John Inman.

Cover Art
© 2015 Maria Fanning.
Cover content is for illustrative purposes only and any person depicted on the cover is a model.

ISBN: 978-1-63216-627-2
Digital ISBN: 978-1-63216-628-9
Library of Congress Control Number: 2014953886
First Edition February 2015

Printed in the United States of America

This paper meets the requirements of
ANSI/NISO Z39.48-1992 (Permanence of Paper).

For John B., who always believed in me.

CHAPTER ONE
ANNIVERSARY

SPENCE'S GOLDEN skin was familiar satin beneath my hands. His fingers buried themselves in my hair as I stroked his lean legs and ran my mouth along his thigh, tasting him as I had tasted him so many times before. And even now, in our fourth year together, he trembled beneath me, just as I knew he would.

Our lovemaking might be choreographed from long experience, but that only meant we knew exactly what the other wanted—what the other ached for. Yet somehow tonight, in the midst of our anniversary celebration and after the consumption of two bottles of excellent Champagne, a nice dinner, and a couple of hours of sweet talk and cuddling on the sofa, our well-rehearsed choreography was about to be tossed out the window. Spontaneity would be unabashedly reinstated, and I'm pretty sure neither one of us saw *that* coming.

Sliding ever upward, I trailed my lips over Spence's hip, kissing, probing, exploring, purposely avoiding the straining cock he was arching his back to place in my path.

Stubbornly, and with infinite amusement, I nudged the heavy shaft of flesh aside with my cheek and dipped my tongue into his belly button instead. He instantly gasped and curled up around my head like a spider in freefall, giggling insanely and grappling with me to withdraw.

"No! I can't stand that." He howled with laughter. "Stop stop *stop*!"

Loving the sensation of his cock throbbing against the side of my face, I snickered maliciously and muttered into a face full of soap-scented pubic hair, "What? What's wrong? This doesn't tickle, does it?"

I fought to stay where I was, but he threw me onto my back and spread his delectable body over mine to hold me down, straddling my chest with his long legs, all the while grinding his cock against my face and smearing a trail of precome across my lips.

I licked it away. "Hmm. Delicious."

He howled even louder when I gripped his ass and pulled him closer, sucking his testicles into my mouth and rolling them around in a game of tonsil hockey.

"Oh, shit," he screamed, laughing so hard he was gasping now. "Don't do that. I hate that!"

It's hard to talk with a mouthful of balls, but I managed. "No, you don't. You love it!"

"It tickles, dammit!"

Slurp, slurp, gobble, snort. "So what's your point, cupcake?"

He spun over me until his head was pointed south instead of north, and the minute he did, he buried his face in *my* crotch and blew into my balls like a playful father blowing into a baby's belly just to make fart sounds. Spence didn't get any fart sounds out of me, but he got a damn good scream, which is probably what he was shooting for anyway.

I lifted my hips off the bed and arched my back into his face. It was a good move, for now I felt his mouth leave my balls and travel up my shaft to take my cockhead into his laughing mouth.

"White boy's dripping," he mumbled around me.

I burrowed my face under Spence's crotch and squirmed my head to the side to get a better angle on his cock but couldn't manage it, so I simply heaved him off me and dumped him on the bed at my side. Now, in a proper 69 position, I went to work in earnest. And so did he.

He groaned as I slid my tongue around his glans, sucking it in, drawing even more precome from his slit for my dining pleasure.

"You taste heavenly," I whispered, clutching his ass and drawing a slow finger over his hole, making him shudder with delight. His legs trembled against me, and I was pretty sure my legs were trembling too.

When he pulled a Linda Lovelace and sucked my dick all the way down his throat and into his gullet, a skill I *still* hadn't mastered, I *knew* my legs were trembling because he pulled them against him and slid his hands over my ass to hold me in place.

"Oh, baby," he breathed over my cock, releasing me now to home in on my balls again. Spence loved tasting my balls. And he knew I loved it too.

Releasing *his* cock, I burrowed under his nuts, lifted his leg high and out of the way, and laid my mouth to his opening.

"Oh Christ, Tyler," he gasped, once more grabbing a fistful of my hair, but he wasn't pulling me away this time. He was pulling me *in*.

I lapped at his asshole like a hungry kid devouring an ice cream cone. Spence shuddered and gasped and bucked against me, and when my tongue tried to work its way in, he arched his back as far as it would go and pulled me even closer.

"You like this," I muttered into him. "No, now, don't deny it. You know you do."

He tugged on my hair until I was beginning to wonder if I would have any left by the time this little session was over. "Oh, for Christ's sake, Tyler, stop jabbering. I don't need a running commentary. But oh, Jesus God yes, do *that* again. Oh Christ!"

He apparently decided he wasn't at the optimal position for what we were doing, so he climbed on top of me, straddling me with his strong golden legs. He eased his ass down gently onto my face and settled in like a mother hen covering a nest of eggs.

And then, as happy as I had ever been in my life, I clutched his thighs to hold him in place and really went to town.

His asshole was delicious. His balls on my chin were heavenly. And when he bent forward to not only expose himself more completely to me, but also to take my cock into his mouth one more time, I thought I'd died and gone to heaven.

He dragged his dick back and forth across my chest, his breath coming in short little gasps, as I continued to burrow my tongue into his welcoming ass. I was confident he liked what I was doing because Spence's viselike legs once again began trembling and shivering and squeezing me in their grip until I started to feel like a filbert in the jaws of a nutcracker. Which reminded me I was hungry.

"I love Chinese food," I mumbled around his asshole.

"*Half*-Chinese," he gasped. "How many times do I have to tell you? I'm *half*-Chinese. Oh God, don't stop, Ty. Please don't stop."

The delicious wet heat of his mouth working away at my cock had me so turned on, I knew if I looked down there I wouldn't see my nuts at all. They'd be absorbed into my body all the way up to my spleen. If my dick got any harder, I'd be able to cut glass with it. Or drive a fucking nail.

My breath stuck in my throat. My back was arched so high I must have looked like a footbridge. I drove my tongue as far up Spence's ass as it would go, and in my excitement I flopped around like a curtain flapping in the wind. "I'm gonna I'm gonna I'm gonna—"

"Hmmm," Spence murmured around me. "Give me your come, baby. Let it go. Fill my mouth. Feed me. Let me drink you down."

Beyond all expectation, my back arched a little higher. I was surprised not to hear a bone snap or see tendons go zinging across the room like rubber bands. With Spence's heavenly ass splayed across my face like a Halloween mask, I felt my balls begin to churn and my cock strained upward as Spence sucked and stroked and slavered and drew me all the way in.

And just as I was about to explode, he scraped his cock over my chest, bumping his balls against my chin when he did, and the next thing I knew he was crying out too. Two seconds later, after a moment of tense silence when all the oxygen seemed to be sucked out of the room for a couple of heartbeats and the two of us froze in an absolute rictus of ecstasy, he suddenly cried out like a banshee at the same time I did.

My come burst forth just as Spence shoved his mouth down over my cock all the way to the root. And at precisely the same moment, his legs clutched me in a grip of iron and his own hot come spilled out across my chest where he was frantically humping me as if he had lost all sense of control, which I'm pretty sure he had.

I quickly grabbed his legs and pulled him up so I could stuff his creamy, heaving cock in my mouth and maybe lay claim to the last few surging jets of come, but I was too late. I got a dribble or two, but the rest was smeared across my chest from my tits to my crotch. Never one to show much restraint or willing to do without, I scraped up as much of his jism as I could and licked it from my fingertips while his throat worked and his hands kneaded and his tongue continued to coax the last drops of come from me.

Still trembling but finally sated, we collapsed against each other and buried our faces into each other's nests of come-splattered pubic hair. Slowly, Spence's cock softened against my lips, and even then I felt more juices oozing out, so I licked them away, shuddering yet again at Spence's trembling response to my continued feeding.

When we were finally able to speak, it was Spence who found words first. His voice was husky and weak. Almost as weak as I felt. "Well, that was new and different."

My heart was still thudding like crazy. "It was wonderful."

"I love you, Tyler Benjamin Powell," Spence crooned, pressing his lips to the base of my cock and pulling me close yet again.

"I love you too, Spencer Walter Chang. More than ever."

We both chuckled at the corny use of our full names, then we let the growing darkness settle around us. I peeked across the heaving terrain of Spence's chest and gazed through the sliding door leading out to the second-floor terrace. The stars were waking in the California sky. A line of palm trees on a hillside in the distance was silhouetted against the last shimmering streaks of an orange sunset.

As we lay there still in a 69 position, Spence stroked the back of my legs with gentle hands and pressed his face into my stomach. "You smell heavenly," he said softly.

I laid my hand to his cheek, and he twisted his head to kiss my palm. "Not tired of me yet?" I asked with a smile. I already knew the answer to that question, or I wouldn't have asked.

"I'll never be tired of you, Tyler. Every day I'm with you, I love you more than the day before. Even when you're a racially insensitive twit and call me a full-fledged Chinaman when you know my mother's as white as you are."

"So you're saying she likes Chinese dick too."

He chuckled. "By all accounts. If you want, I'll ask her next time I see her."

I grinned into his softening cock and another smear of juices spilled across my cheek. I squeegeed it off with my finger and poked the finger in my mouth. "I think you've busted an O-ring. You're still leaking."

He stiffened in my arms.

"What?" I asked. "What's wrong?"

"Where's Franklin?"

At the mention of that name, we both froze.

"Holy crap. He's too quiet. He's probably in the living room, eating your roses."

"Fucking mutt," I growled, "If he is I'll kill him. Those roses you brought me couldn't have been cheap."

"Well…."

"Well what?"

Spence was laughing against my stomach. "Those roses were actually from my sister in celebration of our anniversary. I just changed the card and told you they were from me."

"You cheapass Chinaman."

"There you go again. *Half*-Chinese. *Half*-Chinese. And thank you. But I got you something else."

That perked me up. "You did? What?"

Spence pulled away from me long enough to fish around in the drawer of his nightstand beside the bed. He hauled out a velvet box about the size of a cellphone and, flipping on the light, handed it to me. "It's for both of us actually."

I sat up beside him, and he snaked his arm around my waist, watching my every move.

I flipped open the velvet box and saw two rings, standing side by side, tucked into a bed of black silk. The rings were gold with a band of onyx circling one and a ring of lapis lazuli circling the other. A diamond rested in the center of each. And it was a pretty good-sized diamond too.

"Wedding rings," Spence whispered in my ear. "The blue one is for you. The black one is for me. Unless they sized them wrong. Then it's the other way around."

I couldn't believe it. "Doesn't matter which is which. I love them both."

We had married at City Hall on a whim a year earlier. We told each other we would find the right wedding rings eventually, but work interceded, and we never got around to it. Apparently, Spence had finally grown tired of waiting.

He plucked the lapis ring from the box and said, "Hold out your hand."

I did as he asked, and he slipped the ring over my finger. It fit perfectly.

"Now do me," he said.

So I did. Holding Spence's warm hand in mine, I gently pushed the onyx ring onto his finger, and after a bit of a nudge, it slipped over his knuckle and settled into place.

"They're perfect," I murmured, admiring the sheen of gold on our two hands—one with an inner band of blue, the other a band of black.

I turned and laid my mouth over Spence's. Still clutching hands, our new rings tapping against each other, our kiss seemed to last forever.

Just as I knew *we* would.

How could a love like ours *not* last forever?

FRANKLIN HADN'T eaten the roses, but he had managed to scoot a kitchen chair over to the sink and climb quietly onto the counter while we were in the bedroom doing things Franklin didn't need to know about. Once he was on the counter, he ate every last speck of leftovers, including an entire untouched loaf of garlic bread I had purchased for the *next* night's dinner.

Spence was tugging his underwear on as we stood in the kitchen doorway surveying the destruction.

"Where's the dog?" I growled.

We heard a whimper behind us and spun around.

Franklin stood at the front door with his stomach distended and a piece of tinfoil hanging from the corner of his mouth. His eyes were as big as Ping-Pong balls and he looked like he was about to either poop or barf or explode. Or maybe all three.

I took one look at the poor miserable mutt and said, "DEFCON 4. We have to get him outside. Now!"

Spence and I both took off running, scooping our clothes off the floor where we'd thrown them earlier and dressing so fast I didn't realize until we were done that I was wearing Spence's shirt and he was wearing mine. Even with the time restraints at hand (Franklin was groaning now and looking truly desperate, so the time restraints were growing dire), I had time to relish Spence's scent on the shirt I was wearing. Surprisingly, less than five minutes after our comefest in the bedroom, I again felt my dick twitch in anticipation of whatever *other* sexual escapades might be in store for us on this most extraordinarily romantic anniversary night.

After four years, even the scent of Spence's dirty shirt was enough to drive me crazy.

Unfortunately, if we didn't get Franklin outside pronto, the romantic part of the evening would be over, and we would spend the rest of our anniversary night cleaning up after the dog. And we both knew it.

I grabbed the leash, Spence grabbed the house keys and a fistful of doggy poop bags, and we were out the door like a shot, Franklin dragging us along in his wake.

Franklin did his business less than two steps away from the front porch, so at least the deposit was made in our front yard and not one of the neighbors'. As soon as he had finished, and while Spence was cleaning up the mess, which was spectacular, Franklin did his doggy version of *Cats*, dancing and frolicking around the lawn like he was up for a Tony for best post-poop dance ever. Tongue lolling inside his big toothy grin, he finally settled down, and when Spence was finished with the clean-up and had tossed the nuclear waste in the trash can at the side of the house, we took off down the street for our evening constitutional, Franklin leading the way.

Arm in arm, Spence and I followed.

San Diego is lovely on a summer evening. The air is balmy, the night sky endless. A gazillion stars were just now blinking on as the heavens darkened around them. Only the faintest trace of the red sunset still colored the western edge of the horizon, faintly outlining the city skyline off in the distance.

Spence and I had bought the old Craftsman house in the South Park section of San Diego only two years earlier. The neighborhood was quaint and slowly becoming snootified, as Spence called it, with gentrification gradually transforming the Fifties look of the place into a more modern-day version of itself. As younger, moneyed people began moving in, bringing upscale businesses and maître d'ed restaurants with them, the housing market benefited too, with older homes being spruced up and remodeled and sold for twice the amount they would have pulled in earlier.

I suppose Spence and I were moneyed people too. He was a software engineer, and I was in charge of bookkeeping for a major fast-food chain. Between the two of us, we were pulling down about two hundred and fifty grand a year. Together for four years, married legally for one, and the proud parents of a dog with no scruples whatsoever we had acquired from the Humane Society because we thought it would be wise to have a guard dog—which Franklin most certainly was not—Spence and I were now considering more important additions to our little family. And I don't mean another dog.

"A boy would be nice," Spence said out of the blue, strolling along at my side. I had the impression he was speaking more to himself than he was to me, which didn't stop me from joining in.

"A girl would be nice too," I said. "Or one of each."

Since Spence was holding both the leash and my hand, he quickly dragged the dog and me to a stop, narrowing his eyes and giving me a look that, had he been naked, would have really been a turn-on. "Let's not get carried away," he said, gazing down his nose at me. (He was four inches taller.) His delicately slanted eyes were full of laughter.

I raised my hands in submission. "Fine. One or the other. Not both. But which would you prefer? A boy or a girl? It's a question we should probably settle before we really get the adoption thing rolling."

Spence took exactly two seconds to answer, and therein lies the reason I loved him so much. His answer would have been my answer, only with less blathering and with infinitely more sincerity.

In the moonlight, Spence's face shone soft and sweet as he said, "Whichever one most needs a home."

I nodded and brought his hand to my lips. "Of course."

We walked on beneath the streetlights, Franklin leading the way, happily wagging his tail and sniffing at everything crossing his path. Off in the distance, down the long rolling slope of the city, we could see the sparkling lights of Tijuana shimmering brightly, like a string of jewels laid across the horizon. The night air was scented with woodsmoke from someone's fireplace. Since it was summer and anything but cold, maybe someone else was enjoying a romantic evening, lying cuddled, perhaps, on their living room floor beneath the flickering lights of a fire, naked bodies intertwined, wine glasses forgotten at their side, whispering words of love only the two of them could hear but would never forget.

"God," I said aloud, "I'm having erotic imaginings of *other* people now. I must be feeling romantic tonight."

Spence nudged me with his shoulder. "Good. I like you needy." And for the tenth time since leaving the house, we both looked down at the rings on our fingers.

I leaned in to brush Spence's ear with my lips. Then I pulled away since we were approaching the business section of our little piece of San Diego called South Park. While gays were supposedly accepted, I was still averse to public displays of affection, even if Spence wasn't.

He smiled as I edged away from him, knowing full well what I was doing. "Little Catholic boy is still afraid to be himself."

"You bet," I gently growled. "But don't worry. This little Catholic boy will show you a thing or two later when I get you naked in my bed."

He laughed. "But we did that already."

I cocked an eyebrow high for his benefit. "Yes, and we'll do it again."

"Good," he repeated, and this time it came out in a sexy little purr.

We passed the coffee shop on the corner, and as always the place was packed. Two old men sat at a table outside the front door, playing chess and eating muffins in the spill of light from the window behind them. A yellow Lab curled up at their feet lifted his head to nod at Franklin as we passed, and the two dogs sniffed noses.

At the corner we turned left onto the boulevard. This was our favorite place to stroll. The street was sprinkled with trees that spread their wings above the traffic, in some places reaching all the way across and holding hands over the center line. Now, in the summer, the trees were so heavily foliaged the streetlamps barely lit the sidewalk, giving Spence and me a hushed, shadowy place to once again bump shoulders and brush hands and bandy affectionate words back and forth without the Catholic in me feeling uncomfortable.

Three blocks farther on, we left the boulevard and entered a residential district perhaps half a mile away from our own street. Here, too, the older homes were well cared for, the lawns exquisitely tended, and of all the cars on the street, we didn't see a single clunker. Money had found its way here as well.

Ahead, we could see a split-rail fence beneath a stand of pepper trees, and Franklin began flapping his tail and tugging on the leash. He knew where we were going now, and his eager whimper made that fact crystal clear.

"Come on, come on, come on," Franklin seemed to be saying as he dragged us forward into Doggie Park, his favorite place in all the world.

With a final excited leap, he tore the leash from Spence's hand and took off running.

Spence laughed. "Well, there he goes. No sense of restraint whatsoever."

"Yep," I grinned. "That's our boy."

Spence and I climbed the fence and plopped our asses down on the top rail like a couple of cowpokes, watching Franklin tear around in ever-widening circles over the clipped grass, trailing his leash behind him. He bowled over two Chihuahuas, who were just standing there having a chat, then dove between the legs of a young woman with a Pomeranian. The woman yelped in surprise.

"Sorry!" I called out, but she smiled and waved her hand, letting me know it was okay.

Dog owners are a forgiving breed.

Franklin sniffed the ass of a German shepherd, who didn't seem to mind, then tried to hump a beagle, who did. The beagle snapped at his crotch, and if Franklin hadn't moved when he did, his humping days would have been over forever.

With night having completely fallen and dew settling on the grass, several of the dog owners gathered up their pets, snapped on their leashes, and headed for home. Cars grumbled to life behind us, their headlights stabbing across the lawn. With tires crunching over the gravel parking lot, the owners, with their dogs safely tucked into backseats, took off up the street and disappeared into the night.

Doggie Park was dimly lit by a full moon and one lone security light situated back by the public bathrooms. Since the park was fenced in, we didn't worry too much about Franklin running off. The only way he could escape was through the gate right beside where Spence and I sat perched on the fence.

In the shadows, and with almost everyone gone now, I felt secure enough to take Spence's hand.

"I love the rings," I said, and we both looked down at our hands to admire them again. The diamonds reflected sparks of fire in the moonlight, the bands of gold shone with a softer flame. We had spoken of wedding rings for months, but I had never found a style I liked. As he did with so many other aspects of our life together, Spence took the initiative and found the perfect solution.

His fingers tightened around mine. "I knew they were right the minute I saw them."

"You know me well."

He pulled my hand to his mouth and kissed my ring. "Tyler, I know you better than I know myself. I wouldn't much care about this old life if you weren't here to share it with me. You believe that, don't you?"

No matter how long we had been together, Spence could still melt my heart with a look or a phrase. I swallowed the lump in my throat, and murmured, "Yes. And ditto."

He smiled a wicked smile, his teeth flashing in the dark. "You always did have a way with words."

We both jumped when the young lady with the Pomeranian stepped through the gate at our side and said, "Good night, boys."

"Good night," we said. And Spence added, "Cute dog."

She laughed and scooped the Pom into her arms. "He's the only male in my life who ever made me happy."

Spence pulled me close, as always wearing his heart on his sleeve, for friend or stranger alike. "I know what you mean," he said. "I know *exactly* what you mean."

I elbowed him in the ribs while the woman giggled. Again she said, "Good night," and setting the Pom on the ground, she took off up the street with her little dog leading the way.

We turned back around to see what Franklin was up to, but he was nowhere to be seen.

I whistled. "Franklin! Here, boy."

The park appeared totally deserted. There was not a dog or a human in sight.

Spence cupped his hands around his mouth and called, "Franklin, come here, boy! Time to go home!"

We both gave a worried start when we heard a whimper. It sounded like it came from the bathrooms beneath the security light.

I clapped my hands, which Franklin knew meant big trouble, but we heard nothing. Not even a whimper this time.

Spence and I dropped from the fence and headed across the dew-soaked grass, still whistling now and then, hoping to grab Franklin's attention.

Twenty feet from the public restrooms, we heard voices and a laugh. We stopped in our tracks.

"I thought we were alone," Spence whispered.

"So did I."

I clapped my hands again. "Franklin! Get over here. Now."

This time the whimper was unmistakable as Franklin emerged from the toilet doorway, but only enough for us to see his head. He gave a frightened bark, and it was then I noticed the leash holding him back.

Someone was controlling the leash!

Again we heard whispered voices. Then the flushing of a toilet.

"This isn't good," I mumbled.

"Don't panic," Spence whispered and strode off toward the bathroom door, calling out in his no-nonsense voice, the one he usually reserved for me when I was getting on his nerves.

"Okay, fun time's over, kids. Let loose of my dog so we can all go home." More laughter echoed from the public restrooms, and immediately after the laughter came a voice. And it wasn't the voice of a kid.

"You want your dog, why don't you come on in and get him?"

Spence didn't hesitate. "That's exactly what I intend to do!"

I reached out to stop him, but Spence was too far ahead. He disappeared through the doorway, and I raced to catch up, following along right on his heels.

The stygian blackness of the place took my breath away. The first sound I heard was Franklin growling; then the growl turned to a startled yelp of pain as I heard the unmistakable sound of a boot or a fist striking my dog.

I saw red. "You motherfucker! Let him go."

I swept my hand through the air, trying to find a wall, a stall, Spence—anything to form a frame of reference as to what lay around me. The darkness was absolute but for the gray moonlit opening of the doorway, but even that didn't cast a light inside. In fact it made the darkness more penetrating.

I heard the shuffle of footsteps and Franklin's toenails tapping on the concrete floor. He sounded like he was doing a nervous dance, trying to get away. Franklin growled, but again it was cut short by the sound of a foot or a fist striking flesh. After that, Franklin remained silent but for an occasional whimper.

"Give me the dog!" Spence yelled from somewhere up ahead, and I wondered if he could see whom he was speaking to. I certainly couldn't. But I did feel a body pass beside me from behind, and then another. They seemed to be converging on Spence. Then two hands came out of nowhere and pushed me hard. I landed on my hands and knees in a reeking toilet stall, my head colliding with the commode and making me see stars.

There was a ring of metal. What sounded like a metal rod striking the concrete wall brought me my very first flash of true fear. I struggled to my feet.

"Spence," I cried out. "Run! Get out!"

I heard a scuffle, Spence grunting, and again Franklin yelped, as if in the midst of the battle someone had trod on his foot.

"Fucking mutt," a sinister voice spat.

Someone flicked a cigarette lighter, and the toilet exploded in light. For the briefest of moments before the lighter was knocked from the man's hand, I saw the tableau in perfect clarity. The man holding the light looked Mexican. I could see Franklin's leash wrapped around the hand holding the lighter. The flame was jerking around because Franklin was straining at the leash, trying to get away, jarring the man's hand. The man wore a stocking cap on his head and his face was round and fat, with a horrific black mole on his cheek which I would have made my mission in life to have removed at the earliest opportunity. But maybe psychotic dogsnatchers aren't subject to such aesthetic considerations.

While the fat guy held the lighter aloft to illuminate the scene, three men, one of them Spence, wrestled against the far wall. A tall rangy dude with a straggly moustache clutched an iron bar in his hand like a baseball bat. He swung it with all his force at Spence, missing him completely but knocking a chip of concrete off the wall, which flew across the room and struck me in the cheek. I gasped in surprise and pain.

Still dizzy from striking my head on the toilet, I stumbled into the fray and tried to grab Spence and drag him toward the door. Again a cruel pair of hands shoved me to the floor, and a boot with silver chains on the side of it came out of nowhere, kicking me in the chest.

Gasping for air, I clutched my body as a second kick connected with my hip, making me cry out.

"Leave him alone," Spence screamed. "Goddammit, you're hurting him!"

A mocking, guttural voice came from behind the still-burning lighter. "Look what we got here, boy. A goddamn chink Chinaman and his goddamn faggot boyfriend."

"Leave him alone," I bellowed, and at that precise moment, the flame from the lighter went out as it went flying through the air when Spence threw a roundhouse punch that caught the guy with the mole on the side of the head, knocking him backward into the toilet stall I had just vacated. The cigarette lighter clattered to the floor, sliding off into the darkness.

"Fucker!" someone yelled as I dove forward, trying to reach Spence and drag him away, but I must have grabbed the wrong person. A fist came out of the darkness and slammed into my face, sending me whirling against the wall. My head exploded in pain.

As I slid to the floor, I heard someone gasp, "Enough of this shit. Let's kill these fuckers!"

"No," I bellowed through my haze. "Spence, run! G-get out!"

And just as I tried to grip the wall and pull myself to my feet, I again saw a flash of light. This time it was reflected from the mirror on the bathroom wall as it caught the beam of headlights from a passing car stabbing through the bathroom door. A brief flash of hope it might be a cop was dashed when I heard the car travel on down the street, rap music thumping merrily in its wake.

I flinched when again the metal bar crashed into the concrete wall. Once. Twice. But on the third strike, the sound was different. It was a softer sound. A more brutal, frightening sound. It was the sound of metal on flesh—metal on bone.

A moan tore from Spence's throat that I could never have imagined him making. I thought I knew every sound, every utterance, every whisper he had ever voiced. In anger, in joy, in lust. But this sound was different. It oozed from his body like a spilling of air. Like a loss of hope.

Like a weary acceptance of whatever the fates held in store.

Once more, the metal bar rang out as it struck the floor.

"You missed," a voice sneered. It was the same guttural voice as before. Already I recognized it as coming from the fat guy with the leash.

The next time the metal bar came down, the sound was one I knew I would never, ever forget. It sang out joyfully with the crush of bone, the hammering of flesh. There was a weary release of air, and then the iron bar struck again. And again. A wet sound. A cruel sound.

But that horrible release of air! Was that Spence? Did that sound come from Spence?

"No," I wept, just as another kick struck my forehead. Then another. And darkness swept in.

HOURS LATER—or days—I tried to open my eyes but couldn't. My waking senses were assaulted with the stench of feces, the acrid smell of old urine, or was it new? I vaguely remembered where I was and shuddered.

My cheek lay against the cold concrete floor. I tried to move, but my body would not respond. Was I paralyzed? Was I dead? My lips formed the word "Spence," but no sound came out that I could hear.

As the night air chilled my skin, I reached out my hand to slide it over the floor in the only direction I could. My fingers ached with the movement, a dull pain that stuttered through my body, and I knew they were broken. There, in the still darkness and the growing cold, I felt the softness of Spence's hair brush the tips of my shattered fingers.

And I felt something else—something sticky. It was a spill of blood, already cool to the touch. I don't know how I knew it was blood. I just did. The silence around me was profound. I strained to hear Spence's breathing but heard only the whispered footsteps of a tiny animal, a rat maybe, racing past my head. My body trembled with my own weak struggle for air, for life. I retched and a gout of vomit spilled from my lips. Its comforting liquid heat settled against my cheek.

Spence. Spence.

"No," I pleaded inside my head to a God I didn't believe in. "Not yet. Don't take him from me yet." But the darkness laughed, unheeding, claiming me yet again.

And I knew no more.

CHAPTER TWO
LOSS

COOL FINGERS stroked my forehead. I thought I had never felt a more comforting touch. Somewhere beyond the touch, off in the distance, past the sensation of gentle flesh pressed to mine, I heard a beeping sound. It was like the sound of a truck backing up, the beep that warns pedestrians out of the way. But softer. Not as harsh.

I tried to twist my head into the soothing fingertips on my skin, into that tender, caring touch, but when I did, I realized the touch was no longer there. The fingertips were gone. Or maybe they had never been there at all. A thunderous ache settled over me.

The beeping went on and on. Held captive in the darkness behind my eyelids, and held captive, too, by that horrendous ache raking through me, I tried to imagine what the beeping sound could be. I thought I knew. I was almost sure I did.

But before I could grasp the answer, the ache swept even the question away, leaving nothing behind but pain. It thrummed through my body like a continuous surge of electricity, total and absolute, devouring my every thought.

And it was then my friend the darkness claimed me again.

THE HUM of voices burrowed in, nudging me awake. I felt the dance of my own eyelashes fluttering against my cheek. A cool strip of material, like plastic tubing, lay snug around my neck. When I tried to swallow, the pain was intense, as if my throat were on fire. My hand ached from where it lay pressed to my side. My forearm was being constricted by heavy stone or concrete. I could feel the hardness of it as it lay unyielding against my hip.

A cast. My hand and arm were in a cast. That *must* be what I felt.

But why was my arm in a cast? Was there a car accident? What had happened?

I struggled to open my eyes, but with the first glare of light, I squeezed them shut again. My thoughts were vague, slipping from one to another inside my head like autumn leaves skittering across a lawn, stirred by the wind, never lighting in one place. Never resting. Never making sense.

I tried to calm myself. I wondered absently where the pain had gone, and the moment I did, the pain returned. Everywhere. It screamed through me like a locomotive bursting from a tunnel. Roaring. Angry. Relentless.

I heard a voice cry out. Was that me? Did I make that sound?

Again gentle fingers stroked my cheek.

"Give him something," a voice pleaded, and I wondered if it was me speaking.

"The IV drip will do the trick," another voice intoned.

And once again, the blessed darkness swept me away.

SPENCE, NAKED and beautiful, bucked beneath me. His lean fingers pulled at my hair, pleading with me to take him all the way. I smiled when his juices erupted from his cock, but then I realized something was terribly wrong. Instead of spilling his sweet come into me, he sprayed my throat with fire. Liquid fire. I tried to jerk away but he held me in place as the flames of his orgasm tore into me over and over again. Burning. Burning.

I tried to scream but no sound came out.

My eyes flew open, and the first thing I saw was a red flashing light staring down at me. It stood by… my bed. I was in bed. But it wasn't my bed. It was a bed I had never seen before. This bed had white plastic rails and white sheets, and my legs were tucked under some sort of table down by the foot of it.

Daylight stabbed into my eyes, but I enjoyed the pain. It seemed forever since I had seen the light of day. I teared up against the glare but still enjoyed the sight of thin blinds splayed across a window to my left. It was daylight outside. The sun was shining brightly.

When that old familiar beeping came back to torment my thoughts, I cast my eyes around to learn what it was. It was then I realized the red flashing light and the beeping noise were working in conjunction with each other. And they seemed to be in sync with my own heartbeat. But how was that possible?

I felt pressure on my fingertip, and with concentration, I managed to lift my hand to my eyes. There was a blood-pressure clamp on my index finger. That was what I felt. That was how my heartbeat could be connected to the machine standing by the bed.

When I tried to lift my other hand, I met with resistance. Then I remembered. That was the arm with the cast, and apparently, I was too weak to lift it.

A groan escaped my lips as I twisted my head to look around the room I was in. There was no one else present. No other bed, no other human. No one. Just cabinets, machines, panels.

Where was Spence?

An anguished wail bellowed from me when a storm of memories, one after the other, came screaming in. A metal bar chipping concrete. A dog whimpering in the dark. Mocking laughter and a curse in Spanish. A rat scurrying past my face in the shadows. The reek of piss.

Where was Spence?

I wailed again—an anguished sound that shocked me. It tore at my raw throat like a ragged blade. Only then did I realize I had a trach tube inserted. It felt alien and wrong clamped into me. I tried to grasp it, to pull it out, but I was too weak.

The echo of running footsteps filled the hallway outside my room. My door burst open. The squeak of a trolley. Gentle, insistent hands worked at the tubes that tied me down. Shushing sounds tried to soothe me as the hands did their work.

A drugged dullness slowly settled through me. The room faded. It was the IV drip again. I was beginning to recognize it. I was beginning to welcome it.

My eyelids slowly closed, blocking out the room, the ruckus I had caused. I slept.

I OPENED my eyes and the overhead lights flicked on a moment later. I squinted into the glare. I turned my head to the window. The blinds were open, but there was no daylight shining outside. It was night.

The rustle of fabric caught my ear, and the squeaking of a chair leg being dragged closer to my bed. A hand slid over mine—the hand not entombed in a cast. I almost smiled at the pleasant sensation of flesh against my own. I couldn't seem to remember having felt it for so long.

A familiar voice spoke my name. "Tyler? Tyler? Can you hear me?"

I bit back a sob. It was so grand to hear a familiar voice, even if I couldn't place it. I twisted my head toward the sound, and when I did I realized my throat was free. The trach tube had been removed. Thank God. I swallowed once, twice, just to assure myself I could.

Then I tried to find my voice. It was there somewhere. I knew it was.

A gentle hand clutched my uninjured fingers, awkwardly avoiding the blood-pressure clamp still attached to me. Other fingers wove through mine. I smelled perfume. A familiar scent. Then I remembered. White Linen. Spence bought it for his mother every Christmas. My eyes focused on a face hovering there beside me, and sure enough, it was her. Mrs. Chang. Her hair was bluer than I remembered it. Did women really still put bluing in their hair? And did they still wear it swept back at the sides in crisp finger waves? Or was Mrs. Chang really the last American holdout on bluing and finger waves, as Spence always joked?

Mrs. Chang's eyes were kind as they gazed down at me through bifocals, but there was sadness in her eyes I didn't remember from the times I had seen her before. For a woman who I remembered always laughed at every little thing, the sadness was new. I wondered what had caused it.

The first word I uttered felt like a shard of glass dragged across my throat, but after that, the pain lessened.

"Hi," I said, my whisper little more than a breath of sound. I cleared my throat and tried again as her fingers took a firmer grip on mine. "Mrs. Chang," I said. "It's good to see you." I tried to smile but couldn't seem to accomplish it.

The old woman laid the papery skin of her palm against my cheek. "Welcome back," she answered, which I thought was an odd thing to say. Had I been gone?

Another flurry of muted sound erupted from the other side of my bed. I turned my head, which for some reason caused me to groan, and there, standing by the far wall, was Spence's father. He was unsmiling, as always, but I was used to that. He had never liked me. Spence and I used to joke about it all the time. He didn't like me, and he didn't like the fact that his son was gay. He was a frail little man who still carried a hint of accent from the homeland he had left as a child. But raised in the States, he was American through and through. Right down to his prejudices.

When I rested my eyes on him, he looked slightly startled and quickly turned away to stare through the window into the darkness.

"Tyler," Mrs. Chang said again, pulling my attention back to her. I turned my head to face her, this time without a groan. "Tyler, do you remember what happened? Is there anything you can tell the police?"

"Police?" What would the police have to do with anything? Then shadows began to creep into my mind. Shadows of memory. Franklin on a leash, a woman saying, "Good night, boys," an orange sunset fading into night, a tiny finger of fire illuminating the darkness. A scream. *My* scream.

My heart gave a lurch of fear. "Where's Spence? Why isn't he here? Why am I alone?"

I watched in wonder as two tears slid down Mrs. Chang's cheek. "Oh, honey...."

I heard a sob by the window. Mr. Chang. Mr. Chang was crying.

That sound, more than any other, doused me with sudden terror. I grasped Mrs. Chang's fingers so tightly she gave a little gasp and gently massaged my hand to ease my grip.

"Where's Spence?" I tried to control the panic in my voice, but I could hear it just the same. "Why isn't he here? Was it the car? Was there a wreck?"

Mrs. Chang's tears were flowing freely now, but she had some strength in her. She didn't let them take control. She merely slid in closer and rested her cheek against mine.

"Oh, honey, I—I thought you must have known. Spence... Spence is gone."

And once the words were spoken, her strength collapsed. She wept against me until I felt her tears on my cheek.

I pushed her away with my uninjured hand. I could feel myself tensing in anger. What the hell was she talking about?

Then my eyes opened wide, and I remembered. Doggie Park. The public bathroom.

The iron bar.

"Yesterday," I said, trying to organize my thoughts, trying to remember. "We were walking the dog. Three men—they were waiting for us in the restroom. I—I fell. No, wait. I didn't fall. I was pushed. Franklin whimpered. He was afraid. They kicked him." I still couldn't picture Spence being there, but he must have been. Then I recalled the feel of cooling blood against my fingertips. The scurry of tiny feet on concrete. The rat. The fucking rat.

I gripped Mrs. Chang's hand again, but before I could speak, Spence's dad stood beside me on the other side of the bed looking down. His face had softened. His eyes were wet with tears.

"Spence is gone," Mr. Chang said. "Those three men," he said, "they killed my son. They killed your... husband." And he repeated the first three words he had said to me in months. "Spence is gone, Tyler. He's never coming back."

I found myself smiling. What kind of joke was this? What the hell was he talking about?

"It was only yesterday," I tried to reason. "All that couldn't have happened in one day. Tell me where Spence is. And where's Franklin? Did we get the dog home all right?"

Mrs. Chang tipped my face toward her so I would look at her when she spoke. She had dried her eyes with a Kleenex. It was still wadded up in her hand. I could feel it against my chin.

"Honey, it wasn't yesterday. It was three weeks ago. *Over* three weeks ago now. You've been unconscious. We weren't sure if you would ever wake up at all, but you finally have. I know this is hard for you to understand, but you have to believe us. Spence is gone, baby. Spence is dead. He's buried in Holy Cross Cemetery. He's sleeping there now. He's left us."

The last words were too much for her. Again the tears began to flow, but she didn't shirk away from them. She merely stared at me as those gigantic tears slid down her old withered cheeks.

Only one thought registered on my mind. "It was yesterday. It was only yesterday."

"No," Mrs. Chang whispered. "No, baby. It was almost a month ago."

And it was then that I believed her. My eyes went from her to Spence's dad. They were both weeping now, and when I felt hot tears on my cheeks, I realized I was weeping too.

"He—he's really gone?"

Mr. Chang's voice was cold and angry when he said, "They killed him. They beat him to death like an animal. They almost killed you too. But you survived. We don't know where the dog is. They either took him or he ran away. But you're here. I guess we can be grateful for that much."

He said that last as if perhaps it was my fault I had lived and his own son had not. But I was used to his hatred. It didn't bother me anymore. I focused on Spence's mother instead. She had always been kind. She had always understood about Spence and me.

She understood our love.

"He's really gone?" I asked again, my heart a thudding ache inside me. That ache made the other aches I had experienced feel like child's play. It was like comparing a nuclear bomb to a fistful of firecrackers. I grasped my chest to try to ease the pain. Suddenly I understood how Mr. Chang felt. I began to hate myself for surviving too. It would have been better if Spence had lived. Not me. What good was I to anybody but Spence? Spence had family. Spence had other people who loved him. Spence was *needed*.

Mrs. Chang nodded her old head, jarring another spate of tears from her eyes. "Yes, honey. He's really gone."

"But the funeral," I whispered. "How can he be buried at Holy Cross without a funeral? I never got to say good-bye. I never got to see him one last time."

"We know," she said, her voice shattered with grief. "But we had to let him go, Tyler. We couldn't wait. We had to, because— because we never knew if you were going to wake up at all. Oh God, I'm so sorry, honey, but we had to bury him without you. We had to let him go."

And with that, she dropped her head to the bed and wept with such force I thought her old heart would break. Mr. Chang, rather than reaching out to comfort the woman he had shared his life with, simply turned away from her, from me, and once again stared through the window at the darkened city outside.

I reached out to stroke the old woman's hair with my uninjured hand, and for the first time I realized my ring was gone. The ring Spence had bought me just hours before he… before he….

"His ring," I said. "Was Spence buried with his ring?"

Mrs. Chang forced herself to look at me. Forced herself to bite back her tears. Just to get through this. Just to carry on.

"No, Tyler. He had no jewelry on him. Was there a ring? I don't remember him wearing one."

"Our wedding rings. They were….They were… new."

"The police want to speak to you when you're ready," Mr. Chang said coldly into the windowpane, ripping me from my thoughts. *Freeing* me from my thoughts. From my growing anger.

"Yes. All right," I muttered, staring at my ringless hand.

We had to let him go, baby. We had to let him go. The words kept echoing through my head on an endless reel. Over and over and over again.

Spence was gone.

I closed my eyes, allowing my grief to sweep me away, and needing a place to hide where I could be alone, I pleaded for sleep.

Strangely enough, as if grief was another drug coursing through my IV, it came to release me. Sleep. Folded in its dark arms, I slid away from Spence's memory, and even the memory of Franklin, poor Franklin. They were all gone from me now. Lost.

I was alone.

MY LEGS were weak, but it felt wonderful to walk. The cast hung heavy on my left arm, but that was okay. The nurse said it would come off in a couple of weeks.

The nurse was a man, perhaps my age or a little younger, with skin the color of soot and the brightest eyes and the whitest teeth I had ever seen on a human. He was always smiling.

With a laugh, he teased, "You're lucky. You slept through most of the cast time. You'll only have to put up with it awake for two more weeks. How fortuitous is that?"

I smiled back, but the thought of trying to dredge up a returning laugh made me want to weep. I wondered if I would ever laugh again. All I could think about was Spence lying cold in the ground in a grave I had yet to see. Was a stone up? Were there flowers lying on the freshly turned earth over his head? Did he wonder why I hadn't come to visit?

The nurse's name was Charles. His hands were big and strong and gentle. When he spoke his words carried a faint lisp, as if he had purposely softened the consonants so as not to jolt his patients.

"I think we'd better sit you down," he fussed, seating me on a horrendous orange sofa in the hallway outside my room. "The detective will be here soon. I'll be watching. If you feel you need to go back to bed, just give me a nod, and I'll try to cut the interview short."

"Thank you," I said. And I watched him walk away. In another life I would have found him handsome. Now I just found him kind.

I looked down at my arm. The IV line was gone. They had removed it that morning. There were puncture marks above my wrist where they had tapped my vein, and the puncture marks were beginning to itch. I raised my hand to touch the scar in my throat where they had performed the tracheotomy. It felt rough and pebbly against my fingertips. Unfamiliar. That wound was also itching. But neither battle wounds itched as much as the plaster cast around my arm. That fucker drove me crazy. Still, what with all the itching going on, I supposed it meant I was on the mend.

And my heart? That was another story altogether, for an overwhelming sadness seemed to weigh down on me every minute of every day. I wondered what would become of the child Spence and I could not now adopt. Would that child find another home? Would he or she find someone to love them as much as Spence and I would have loved them? Or was that just one more life ruined by the three men who came at us in the dark? Did those three men know the misery they had caused? Did they even care?

Every time I thought of them waiting in the darkness, luring Spence and me forward, an anger took control of me that made all my physical problems seem like nothing. I realized I had never known hate before. Not really. Not like the hate I knew now. I seethed with it. I burned. For the hundredth time that day, I closed my eyes against it, trying to rein it in. Slowly, in the darkness behind my eyelids, I felt my anger wane. I felt my one good hand unclench in fury.

My fingertip continued to stroke the trach scar at my throat. It would be there for the rest of my life. All the scars would be with me from this day forward. Every fucking one of them. Inside and out. The only thing that wouldn't be with me was Spence.

We had to let him go, baby.

My thoughts were interrupted by footsteps approaching. I clutched my hospital gown more securely around me and readied myself for my first interview with the police. It was already a month after the fact, but I had only fully awakened two days before. I wondered if there was anything I could tell them they didn't already know. My memories of that night were so fractured. I remembered almost nothing.

Only the feel of congealing blood against my aching, broken fingers. The ring of metal on concrete—and on flesh and bone. Those memories were still in place. I suspected they always would be.

"Hello, Tyler. I hope I haven't kept you waiting."

It wasn't what I had expected to hear. On the cop shows, they weren't that polite.

I tried to ignore the tremor in my voice. The tremor was from weakness—I was still weak—but it was also from fear. This interview scared me. I wasn't sure why.

"I think maybe I'm the one who's kept *you* waiting," I said. "For almost a month, I guess." I stuck out my hand and made a motion to stand up, but he waved me back onto the sofa.

"Let's not stand on ceremony," he smiled. "Instead of you coming up here, why don't I just come down there." And he plopped his ass down beside me. Once he was comfortably situated, he took my hand just as I had been about to do to him.

He gave my hand a good shake. "Detective Martin. Glad to meet you, Tyler. There now," he said, "wasn't that easier?"

"Thanks," I mumbled. "I guess I'm still a little puny."

Detective Martin was lanky and gave off an air of competence. A tall beanpole of a guy, he studied me with honey brown eyes tucked between long black lashes. He looked tired. There were dark smudges under his eyes, and his brown hair was sort of a mess. He needed a haircut, for one thing. The back of his neck needed shaving. So did his cheeks, but not as badly. He wore a suit so rumpled I was tempted to ask if he had slept in it. Smiling at me, he rested his hands on his knees. Those hands were big and capable looking, with a brush of dark hair sweeping across the backs of them and in between the first and second knuckles of the fingers. His fingernails were cut blunt, and one knuckle was scabbed over as if he had been in a fight. Occupational hazard, maybe.

He couldn't have been much older than me, and I suppose that's what surprised me most about him. That and the fact he was really quite handsome, in a careless, unintentional, loosely jointed way. Sort of like a big kid who hadn't yet grown into his body.

But the brown eyes were kind, and that, more than anything, eased my fear.

He cleared his throat, as if he thought he should get the basic stuff out of the way first. "I'm sorry about what happened to your lover. I know this can't be easy for you."

Something about the way he said it rubbed me the wrong way. "Spence wasn't my lover. He was my husband. We were legally married." I said it with a certain amount of in-your-face bravado, as if daring him to say something homophobic.

But I knew immediately I had taken the wrong tack.

He shifted around on the sofa to better face me. His hand came to rest on my shoulder. "Tyler, I understand the two of you were married. I'm not trying to belittle what you guys had. I understand you loved each other. I'm not judging you for that. My job is just to help you get through this by finding the men who took Spence from you and who left you like this." He nodded at the cast on my arm, the crappy hospital gown I was wrapped up in. "Don't think I'm one of the haters. I'm not. I'm here to help you."

I felt a blush rise to my cheeks. "I—I'm sorry. I know you are here to help. I don't know why I'm being so defensive."

Detective Martin gave me a frown, as if he couldn't quite believe what I had just said. "Tyler, you have every right in the world to be defensive. You have every right in the world to be angry. But what I need you to do for me now is focus some of that anger on helping me find the ones who did this. Think you can do that?"

I sucked in a deep breath. "Yes. I can do that, Detective Martin."

His face softened. "I think this will go faster if you knock off the Detective Martin stuff. Just call me Chris. All right? I'll call you Tyler, you call me Chris."

I nodded. "All right. Chris as in Christopher?"

He smiled. "No. Chris as in Christian. Okay?"

"Okay."

He pulled a notepad from his inside jacket pocket and plucked a pen from his shirt pocket.

"Let's get started then, shall we?"

And once again I nodded.

AN HOUR later, Chris flipped the notepad closed.

"When do you go home?" he asked.

"Tomorrow, I hope."

"Is there anyone there to help you?"

"I don't need anyone to help me. I'll be fine on my own." *On my own.* The words echoed through my head. Out of nowhere, tears started flowing. I tried to cover my embarrassment by jabbering questions at the man who was sitting beside me and trying, for kindness' sake, to ignore my tears.

"I guess I didn't help you much," I said, dragging the sleeve of my robe over my face.

Chris smiled kindly at me. "If you did guess that, your guess would be wrong."

I sniffed. "Really?"

Again he flipped over his notepad. "You've given me several facts we didn't know before. The most important is the partial description of two of your assailants. The fat guy with the mole on his face and the tall, skinny guy with the ratty little moustache. And by the way, the fat guy probably smokes, that might come in handy too."

That took me by surprise. "How do you know he smokes?"

Chris tapped the notebook with a fingertip. "Why else would he be carrying a cigarette lighter?"

"Oh, yeah."

"But most of all, Tyler, you told me about the rings that were stolen. The wedding rings. That was news to us, and they may be the very pieces of evidence we need to tie things up. If they try to hock the rings, we'll know about it within twenty-four hours. You're sure neither of you was carrying anything else on you besides the house key, which we found on the floor by your feet?"

"I'm sure," I explained again. "We ran out of the house so quickly we didn't even grab any money. At least I didn't, and I'm pretty sure Spence didn't either."

"One more thing," he asked. "Is the dog microchipped?"

"Yes."

He nodded sagely, as if the fact that Franklin was microchipped was the most important piece of evidence there was. But I didn't buy it for a second.

"So what are the chances of your finding them?" I asked. "The killers. What are the chances of your bringing them in?"

The detective didn't seem too happy with my question. I guess I couldn't really blame him.

"Almost a month has passed since the crime, and that's never a good sign. But now that you're awake and have given us a little more to work with, I think we've got a shot at cracking this. I hate to break this to you, but I'll need more cooperation from you than this one little interview. I have books of mug shots for you to go through as soon as you're up to it, and I want you to try to remember everything you can about that night. Everything." He dug in his coat pocket again and extracted a business card, pressing it into my hand. "Here's my card. You can call me any time you want, day or night, if you think of something. Or even if you just need to talk." He chuckled. "I don't sleep much, so it's not like you'd be keeping me awake."

I looked at the card. Detective Christian Martin. Homicide. The lettering blurred when my tears started burning again.

I reached out and took his hand, expecting him to pull away from such a personal touch, but to my surprise, he didn't. He simply sat there beside me on that god-awful orange Naugahyde couch, holding my hand and waiting for what it was I wanted to tell him.

I finally got the words out. "I want you to get these guys for me, Detective. Spence was a wonderful man. If you had known him, you would have liked him. I know you would. Please don't let these animals get away with killing him like a dog in the street. Please. Please don't let that happen."

Detective Christian Martin, Homicide, held my hand between both of his and soberly studied my face. If he was horrified by my tear-filled eyes and my snotty nose, he didn't let it show.

"Don't worry, Tyler. We'll get it done. I promise."

I exhaled a long shuddering breath and gently pulled my hand away. "Thank you," I said.

And before the silent tears turned to racking sobs, embarrassing me even further, I heaved myself to my feet and walked away.

At the door to my hospital room, I turned to wave good-bye, but the detective was already gone.

I wondered if he would keep his promise.

CHAPTER THREE
HOME

I STOOD in front of the wide walk-in closet in the master bedroom and stared at Spence's clothes hanging there. Spence's side of the closet was neatly arranged. Even his shoes were perfectly lined up, toes out, heels to the wall, as if the photographer from *Closet World* was scheduled to pop in for a photo shoot.

As always, my side of the closet looked like someone had tossed a hand grenade in it.

It was only my third day after waking from a twenty-four-day coma to find myself a widower, and I was already cried out. As I stared at Spence's clothes, I wondered where the rest of my tears had gone. All I felt was empty. My throat was still raw and sore from the tracheotomy. My broken fingers and wrist still wailed every time I moved the wrong way. My legs and back still ached from being immobile so long. My brain was stuck in reverse, continuously recalling everything about the past and registering almost none of the stimuli bombarding me in the present.

I heard the tap of approaching high heels, and Spence's sister, Janie, came up beside me to snake an arm around my waist. She rested her head on my shoulder as we both stared into the closet. Into the past. A past now forever gone, just as pasts always are.

"You shouldn't be thinking about this now," Janie said softly, and I nodded.

"I know."

Janie Chang had graciously driven me home from the hospital since the doctor wouldn't let me take a cab as I requested. Too impersonal, he had said, not understanding that *impersonal* was exactly what I needed. So I had said good-bye to my hospital room, tossed the get-well cards into the wastebasket, and left instructions for the flowers sent by friends and family back East to be distributed any way the nurses saw fit. I never looked back as I left the place where I had slept away the last three and a half weeks of my life. I sat in the hospital-ordered wheelchair as Janie wheeled me out. I was wearing sweats, which Janie had retrieved from the house since I refused to wear the clothes I had been attacked in.

Janie took my hand and tugged me toward the kitchen. "I've made you a sandwich," she said, so I followed. Not because I was hungry, but because I was too tired to argue.

Janie prattled on and on as she led me through the house. She was a decade older than Spence and looked considerably more Chinese. She had never married, was a little on the pudgy side, and taught piano and art at the junior college downtown. She had long dark hair that had only recently begun to gray at the temples and which she stubbornly refused to do anything about. The only good thing about Janie's prattling was it required no response. Janie never seemed to expect it.

Notorious in the Chang family for being unable to cook, Janie had prepared me a tuna sandwich and opened a can of pork and beans. Apparently, she had attempted to hide the mediocrity of the food by putting it on my best china and placing one of my best damask napkins at the side of it. She had poured a serving of milk into a Looney Tunes jelly glass. Bugs and Elmer had never been in better company.

While I pretended to eat—with one hand, since the other was still encased in plaster—Janie excused herself and clattered off to the back of the house to make a call on her cell phone.

Finding myself relatively alone for the first time in days, I breathed a sigh of relief.

I sat at the table with one hand in my lap, the other suspended in my sling. Except for the faint hum of Janie's voice rattling away in the background, the house was disconcertingly silent. I could never remember it being this quiet. No laughter, no music, no tippy-tapping of Franklin's toenails as he ran around all over the place. No calling out from Spence telling me we were going to be late. Or what did I want for dinner? Or demanding a date night—as if he ever had to demand one at all.

The house even *smelled* unused. In fact, it smelled the way it had when Spence and I first bought it. Empty. Unlived-in. Vacant. I guess the living—meaning Franklin, Spence, and me—had all been absent for too long. Even the air in the house had grown stale from lack of use.

Looking down at the corner of the kitchen floor next to the door leading into the basement, I saw Franklin's empty dog dish. The water in his water dish had evaporated long ago, leaving a dull film behind. I clutched my chest to fend off the sudden pang of heartache, wondering if Franklin was lost on the streets, starving, injured, alone and afraid. God, I hoped not. I couldn't bear to think of him that way.

Turning to peer into the dining room, I realized Janie's yellow roses, the roses Spence had jokingly tried to pass off as his gift to me, were dead and brown. Withered petals were sprinkled across the dining-room table, still lying where they had fallen. I was pretty sure the faint reek of decomposition I smelled came from the spoiled water in the vase. It was so like Janie to serve a tuna sandwich on the best china, place it on the kitchen table, then leave a rotting spray of roses to stink up the house on the dining-room table less than fifteen feet away.

In front of me, past the jelly glass with Bugs and Elmer on it, sat a pile of mail that had accumulated during my stay in the hospital. I could tell by the color and shape of the envelopes that much of it consisted of greeting cards. I wondered if it had been confusing for my friends to decide what sort of card to send. Should they purchase a sympathy card to offer their condolences on the loss of my husband while ignoring the fact that I had been pounded into a coma, or was it more socially responsible to shoot off a get-well card for my benefit and ignore the fact that Spence had been beaten to death like an animal, leaving yours truly all alone? Or should they buy both cards and cover all the bases?

Tough choice.

I picked up the pile of letters and cards and bills and dumped the lot of it in the wastebasket beside my chair. Then I bent down and fished it all out again. There were probably bills in there and other important stuff. I would sort it out later. Life goes on, after all.

Not that I particularly wanted it to.

Let's face it, I was exhausted. Sadness and grief and pain had sapped every ounce of courage and strength from me. All I had left was anger. And that was burning brightly all the way down to the bone. I seethed with it. I was pretty sure, in fact, that anger was the very thing keeping me alive. Anger and a need to strike back.

I stared through the kitchen window, trembling with hate.

A clatter of high heels heralded Janie's return. She stood behind my chair and rested a hand on my shoulder.

"You're not eating."

"I will."

"Is it all right? Maybe you'd like something else."

"Everything is fine. Thanks, Janie."

She ran cool fingers, *piano* fingers, through my hair. "You need a haircut."

"I know."

"I have a class in forty-five minutes. Will you be okay on your own?"

"Yes. Thank you."

"I'll stop by later to—"

The thought of her returning made my weariness worse. "No, please, Janie. You've done enough. I need some time to myself. I'll call you in a couple of days. All right?"

"If you're sure." She sounded relieved.

"I'm sure."

She bent and gave me a peck on the cheek. I lifted my good hand and patted the side of her face, wishing she would go.

"Okay, then," she said, "try to get some rest."

Leaning in closer, she whispered in my ear. "I want those fuckers caught, Tyler. I want them to pay for what they did to my brother. And what they did to you. If there is any way I can help make that happen, let me know."

I nodded, mute, pleading silently for her to leave. She finally did, gathering up her purse and the sweater she'd tossed on a chair. After a final peck on the cheek and a lingering caress of my unkempt hair, she clattered her way to the front door. On the way she walked right past the reeking, rotting flowers on the dining-room table without giving them a glance or a thought.

As soon as the front door clicked shut behind her, I picked up the plate with the tuna sandwich on it and flung it into the sink ten feet away. The china shattered and the sandwich splattered the window. I picked up the bowl of pork and beans and calmly sat there, realizing what a mess I would make if I threw that too. With a sigh of resignation, I carried it to the refrigerator and calmly placed the dish inside. Then I walked back to the bedroom and stood before the walk-in closet, eyeing Spence's clothing and wondering how I was ever going to get along without him.

I finally closed the closet door to block out the sight of everything that had ever meant anything to me in my life—Spence, Spence's things, Spence's love—and stared instead at my reflection in the mirrored closet door.

The bruises on my face were gone but for a faint tinge of green around my right eye. There were benefits to being in a coma for close to a month. I hadn't had to deal with seeing how I looked after being beaten to a bloody pulp. I didn't have the memory of all the pain that came with the beating because I had slept through it. I recalled hazy moments of misery here and there, but they had left no lasting impressions.

The only pain I still carried with me from the beating was that of my broken fingers. They had been stomped on, the doctor had coolly informed me, and I remembered the motorcycle boot with the thin silver chains dangling off the side of it—the boot that came out of the darkness and kicked me in the chest. Had it been the same heavy boot that smashed my four fingers in one incredible act of cruelty and malevolence? Or had one of the other attackers done that? I supposed I would never know.

My hatred flared hotter at the thought—at the possibility—of never knowing the truth. I closed my eyes until the feeling passed.

Opening them again, I stared at my reflection once more as I listened to the silent house echo an empty song of mourning around me.

With my arm entombed in plaster, resting in the sling, the sweatpants and T-shirt Janie had brought for me to wear, the greenish bruise on the side of my face, the untended hair, the red eyes, I had to admit I looked like shit. But I didn't care. There was something I had to do.

Studying my cast, I realized I would never be able to drive.

I rifled through the dresser drawer to scrounge up some money, took a credit card as well, just in case the cash wouldn't be enough, and picked up my cell phone to call a cab.

I stood inside the front door until the cab pulled up out front. Then, with racing heart, I locked the house behind me and limped down the sidewalk toward the taxi.

I had to see Spence. And I understood the need of that. I did.

What I didn't understand was the terror I felt stepping outside my front door. Without the walls of my house around me, I felt defenseless. Unprotected. That fear was new. But I would deal with it later.

I clutched my cast protectively to my chest and climbed into the cab.

"Holy Cross," I said to the driver, and he flipped the meter. All business.

HOLY CROSS Cemetery was just off the 805 freeway. I had never been to the place in my life. At the cemetery gates the cab driver asked, "Which way?" and it dawned on me I had no idea where the grave was located.

I pointed to an admin building off to the left. "Take me to the office. I'll have to ask."

The driver cast me a look through the rearview mirror. The look was less than stellar.

To appease the guy, I said, "Don't worry. You can keep the meter running."

He found a parking space, and I ducked through the door marked Office. Inside I found a middle-aged Latina with a name tag that read Isabela Herrara.

"Can I help you?"

I told her what I needed, and she checked a ledger filled with the names of dead people. I choked back a sob to think that Spence's name was in there among the others.

"Ah, yes, he's recent. Here it is." She led me to a map on the wall and showed me how to find the grave by traversing a maze of paved lanes. Then she handed me a smaller Xerox of the same map after marking Spence's grave with an *X*.

I nodded my thanks and hustled back to the cab, trying to maintain control, trying not to think too much about what I was doing. Trying not to cry. Trying not to remember the words, *Ah, yes, he's recent.*

I gave the driver the map and muttered, "*X* marks the spot."

He simply nodded. After studying the map for a moment, we took off, hopefully in the right direction. Apparently it was. A few moments later, he pulled to the curb and, after checking the map one more time, pointed to the right into a field of tombstones. "Six graves down," he said in a bored voice.

But already I could see the rectangular scar on the lawn about fifty feet away. The lumpy, poorly laid sod.

With my mind determinedly blank, I again clutched my cast to my chest as I angled myself out of the cab and stumbled awkwardly over the spongy lawn. The cemetery smelled of freshly cut grass. Off in the distance, I could see the Coronado Bridge, arching across the bay to Coronado. I realized it was a beautiful spot to spend eternity. Not that that made me feel any better.

By the time I reached the grave, tears were coursing down my cheeks. I chewed on my lip to stop myself from screaming in anger as I stared down at the rectangle of disturbed earth, unmarked by anything but a flimsy metal marker holding a slip of paper with Spence's name on it. There were flowers in a glass vase propped up beside the marker, but they were as dead as the ones on my dining room table.

I whispered into the summer air, "I'll get you a stone, Spence. I promise. First thing."

My only answer was the hum of bees. The distant warbling of a mockingbird. The rustle of fronds in a palm tree back near the taxi.

I looked back and saw the cabbie standing by his car door smoking a cigarette. He wasn't watching me. He was looking the other way.

"I'll be back as soon as I can drive, Spence. A couple of weeks. But I'll get them started on the stone right away." Again I said, "I promise." As if the corpse lying six feet underground could actually hear what I was saying.

The words *I love you* were on my lips, ready to be spoken, but somehow I couldn't utter them.

I simply turned away and, blinded by tears, stumbled back to the cab.

The cabbie flipped his cigarette into the grass, closed the door behind me, and climbed into the front seat.

"Home?" he asked.

And seeing him watching me in the rearview mirror, I brushed the tears from my cheeks and tried to put on a businesslike face.

"No," I said. "Go back to the cemetery office. There's something I have to attend to." The stone. I had to buy Spence a stone.

The cabbie nodded, glancing at the still-ticking meter. "All right."

Thirty minutes later the gravestone was ordered, and the cab was once again pulling through the cemetery gates, this time back to the world of the living. I kept my eye on the bare patch of earth covering Spence's grave until I could no longer see it.

Then I turned back into myself and wondered what I would do next. With the day. With my life. The driver remained silent the rest of the way home.

I LAY in bed as sunset smeared the sky outside my bedroom window. It was the same sort of sunset Spence and I had looked out on the last night we were together. I reached up and twisted the rod to close the vertical blinds against the sight of it. Against the memory.

I had been lying awake for over two hours, not sure what to do and too weary to do much anyway. My cock was hard because I was remembering how Spence and I had spent those last few hours we shared together. The feel of his skin beneath my hands. The taste of his come surging across my tongue. The way he had cried out at the moment of ejaculation. The same as I had. The familiar aftermath. The cuddling, the quiet words of love, the gentle way he held me as our hearts slowed and the sweat dried on our skin. The giving of the rings. The laughter.

The walk to Doggie Park.

With a sudden thought, I stood and tore the wrinkled bedspread aside with my good hand. Clumsily, because of the cast, I sprawled out face down on Spence's side of the bed to smell his scent on the sheets. But with an ache of loss almost as intense as grief, I realized the scent of him was gone. I could smell only fabric softener and detergent. Someone, Janie maybe, had changed and washed the sheets while I was in the hospital, erasing my last personal touch of the man I had loved and who had loved me in return.

"No!" I railed at the silent house.

Once again, fury raged through me. At Janie. At fate. At the fuckers in the park.

I reached out for something to strike, something to throw, but the jangle of the telephone on the desk in the corner brought me to my senses.

I waited for the answering machine to pick up. On the fifth ring, it did. The familiar voice sounded metallic over the speakerphone. I almost didn't recognize it.

"Tyler, this is Chris Martin. I was just at the hospital and they told me you were released. Are you there? If you are, I need to speak to you."

Reluctantly, I picked up the phone. "Yes, Detective. I'm here."

"Ah, good. How are you feeling?"

"Fine," I said. My voice sounded bland even to my own ears. "How are you?"

"Eh. Listen, I brought some mug shots to the hospital for you to look at, but now that you're home, I thought I would bring them over there. That be all right? If you don't want company, I can just drop them off."

I wondered. Did I want company? "Sure, Detective. Bring them over." With the blinds drawn, the house was almost dark. Night was moments away. "What do you do? Work around the clock?"

I thought I detected a groan in his voice when he said, "Pretty much. I'll be there in five."

"You know where I live?" I asked.

And the groan in his voice intensified. But it was a friendly groan. At least I imagined it to be. "Tyler, I know everything about you there is to know." And he ended the call.

I didn't have time to change out of my sweats, but I did go to the bathroom to splash water over my face and brush my teeth. I took a swipe at my hair with a hairbrush, and by the time I switched on the interior lamps and flicked on the porch light, Detective Martin was climbing the steps toward my door.

"Nice house," he said, juggling a stack of what looked like photo albums and three bags of fast food. I mumbled a "thank you" as I ushered him through the door, and the aroma of hamburgers and french fries almost knocked me off my feet. "Figured you can't drive, and since I was starving, I thought you might be hungry too. Brought enough for both of us." He indicated the familiar clown logo on one of the paper bags. "I even purchased dinner from the company you keep the books for. Didn't figure you'd want to be eating your competitor's stuff. Professional loyalty and all that."

"Uh, gee," I stammered, knowing he was making a joke, but still surprised by his kindness in bringing me dinner at all. "Thanks."

Detective Martin—or Chris—was still wearing the same wrinkled suit he had worn the day before. As he passed directly under the porch light I noticed a pretty good sprinkling of hair on the suit, and it wasn't the detective's.

"You must have a cat," I said.

Chris looked down at himself and softly cursed as he tried to hold on to everything he was carrying and still brush off the front of his jacket. "Yeah, I do. Fucking Waldo," he growled, but it wasn't a mean growl. Just resigned. Love/hate relationships with pets I understood perfectly. Anyone who had spent any time with Franklin would pretty much have to.

Being hindered by the cast on my arm, I wasn't much help to the detective as he crossed the living room and finally dumped everything he was carrying on the coffee table.

"I'm sorry," he said, at last having two free hands to give his suit coat a good slapping to dislodge the cat hair, after which he did the same to the front of his slacks. "I don't usually make this bad an impression. At least, I don't think I do."

His words shocked me. "Umm. You just brought the perp book, or whatever it's called, all the way out here to me instead of making me cab it down to the police station, and on top of that, you brought dinner along with it. I wouldn't exactly call that making a bad impression. Take off your jacket, Detective. And your shoes, if you want. Get comfortable. You look about worn out, if you don't mind my saying so."

That brought a blush to his cheeks. "Yeah, well, it's been a long day. But thanks. I'll take you up on that offer. Where do you want to eat?" He motioned to the coffee table. "Here?"

"Here's fine," I said. "Sit down. I'll get some napkins."

"Don't bother," he said, pulling a stack of paper napkins from one of the bags. "We've got plenty."

I was rather taken aback by the sudden realization that I liked the man. He seemed like a nice guy. And under different circumstances, I might have considered him friend material. Spence would have too, maybe even throwing in a few jibes in my direction about how cute the detective was, which in my eyes he really wasn't at the moment, but I suspected Spence would have thought he was. In Spence's opinion, kindness was as sexy as hunkiness. And maybe it was to me too.

But while I accepted the fact that I found Detective Martin likeable, I also knew he was the enemy. I expected things from him—let's not beat around the bush, I expected *arrests*—and if they weren't forthcoming, I knew I was going to be pissed.

The detective drew a blank expression. "I forgot drinks."

"No problem. I have soda." I strode on weary, weak legs to the kitchen, pulled out a two-liter bottle of Coke from the fridge, and grabbed two glasses from the cupboard, doing my own little balancing act since I only had one good arm to work with. I returned to the living room with my load and placed it on the coffee table as Chris and I lowered ourselves onto the sofa.

"I think you'll have to pour," I said, and he nodded while he finished pulling off his jacket and draping it over the back of the couch. He wore a wrinkled pinstriped dress shirt with sweat stains in the armpits and had what looked like a ketchup stain on his tie. The tie hung loose around his neck. He seemed to realize he wasn't looking his best.

"Sorry," he said, stroking the five o'clock shadow darkening his chin. "I told you it'd been a long day. There was even a pretty good foot chase in the middle of it, so I'm not in pristine condition."

"Catch your man?" I asked.

And to my surprise, he went for humor, shining an imaginary badge with his shirt cuff and looking all cocky for my benefit. "Yes, I did. Caught him cold. The lowlife fuck." Then he went back to reality, digging through one of the fast-food bags. "Taco or hamburger? Or several of each. Your choice. We've got plenty."

"Both," I said, and he nodded as if to say, "Good."

We sat there, companionably enough, through the first few minutes of sating what appeared to be a raging hunger on both our parts. When the feeding frenzy began to die down, Detective Martin seemed to feel there were things to be said. He eyed me carefully, but there was sincerity behind his gaze.

"So how are you doing, Tyler? Really. How are you feeling?"

I swallowed hard, not expecting the question. "I'm okay. Just—" I looked around the room like I had never seen it before. "Just trying to get used to a silent house, Detective."

"Chris," he said. "Call me Chris."

I nodded. "Right. I forgot." I laid the sandwich aside and took a sip of soda. "I guess I'm not used to being alone. I miss Spence, of course. And Franklin."

"Franklin's the dog," he said.

"Yeah. He was kind of a nitwit. The thought of him lost on the streets is killing me. I hate to think of him… suffering. Or hungry."

"He may still turn up," Chris said. "You said he was microchipped."

"I know." I adjusted the cast in the sling until my hand ached a little less. I stared into the unlit fireplace simply because I couldn't bear to look at a living face. But the words I spoke were like the sudden lancing of a putrid wound. I needed to say them. To *somebody*. I needed to let out the pus. "It's hard knowing Spence is gone. You may not understand this, but no one—no one—has ever loved me the way he did. And no one will ever love me that way again. It was a once-in-a-lifetime thing, Detective. I mean, Chris. I'll never have that happiness again, and I know it. That's a sobering realization."

I shyly turned to face him to see what he was thinking. His honey-colored brown eyes were studying me with concern. When our eyes came together, he gave me a sympathetic smile. His hand came out to touch my shoulder.

"I know it must be hard for you," he said. "But don't give up on life just yet. No one really knows what lies in store for us. Love always seems to come along when we least expect it. You're going through a grieving period now. Try not to let it scar you for the rest of your life. And if it's any consolation, I think we have a pretty good shot at finding the people who did this to you."

"Do you really?" I asked, not believing him for a second. "It's been almost a month already. What big break in the case do you think is going to turn up now?" I tried to keep the sarcasm out of my voice, but I knew I wasn't doing a very good job of it.

Chris seemed to understand my anger. Being in his line of work, I supposed he would. "There was a lot about the attack we didn't know until three days ago, Tyler, when you woke up and started talking to us. The way I see it, the investigation didn't really start a month ago when the assailants struck. It started the minute you opened your eyes and told us what had happened. That's when this case really got moving. It's not a cold trail. It's not a cold case. Hell, the investigation is just beginning. Give us a chance. Don't give up hope yet. All right?"

I stared at his eager, honest face, at the compassion in his tired eyes, at the determined slant of his broad shoulders. For the first time, I realized there was a gun in a shoulder holster strapped to his side. I couldn't believe I hadn't seen it there before.

"All right," I said, as weary and downhearted as I had ever been in my life. I let my eyes trail from the gun to the stack of photo albums he had placed on the floor beside the coffee table. "If we're done eating, maybe I should be looking at your pictures now."

"They're booking photos. Mug shots," he said with a gentle smile. "We call them mug shots."

"All right then. Mug shots." I gave him a tiny smile back.

The smile felt good on my face. Chris must have enjoyed the sight of it as well. He stared at it for a long moment with an odd, quizzical expression. Then, as if remembering what he was there to do, he pushed away the mess of sandwich bags and napkins and all the other detritus from our hastily arranged meal and placed the first of the photo albums in front of me on the table.

Before he opened it for me, he said, "I hope you're still trying to remember everything about that night you can. We've canvassed the neighborhood but we need your help too. As you start feeling better, maybe your mind will open up a little more. Maybe more memories will start seeping in. About the people you saw as you and Spence were walking to the park. Or more importantly, the people you saw at the park itself. People who might remember seeing three men go into the restroom. People who might even have been frightened by the attack they knew was going on and fled the scene not wanting to get involved. Make notes if you have to. Maybe it will keep your thoughts straight."

Again I studied his eager face. "You expect a lot," I said.

His eyes narrowed slightly. He didn't like my comment. "And so should you," he said quietly. "I saw what they did to you, Tyler. I was at the hospital when they brought you in. Before the case was even given to me."

I blinked back surprise. "How could that be? You saw me? You were there?"

"It happens all the time, actually. I was investigating a domestic violence case. A woman beaten to within an inch of her life. We had the husband in custody and I was waiting for the wife to wake up and tell me what we already knew, which, by the way, she never did. She died in the emergency room. But while I was waiting, I saw them bring you in. I watched as they treated you." He reached out and eased my shirt collar aside with his long, capable fingers to expose my tracheotomy scar. "I watched through a window when they did the tracheotomy so you could breathe. They suspected you were concussed, with a skull fracture, and weren't entirely sure you'd make it. But you did. You were lucky that night, Tyler. You could very easily have died."

I sat there listening to him, speechless. No one had explained to me how close to death I had come. Not my doctors, not the nurses, not Spence's family. No one.

"And you were there all along," I said, as if I still couldn't believe it.

"Yes. I've been working your case since the very first night. I know you aren't aware of that, but it's true. I was there when the techs worked the crime scene. I was at the morgue to view your partner's autopsy. While the medical examiner worked, I tested for DNA under his fingernails, hoping he might have scraped one of his assailants with his nails. The only substance I found was semen. It was from you."

I jumped. "That night, we…. It was our anniversary. Just before we left the house, we made love." I studied the detective's face. "You saw Spence at the morgue?"

It was Chris's turn to stare into the empty fireplace. "Yes. I saw what they did to him. If it's any consolation, he died instantly. He didn't suffer."

I nodded. "I know. The doctor told me." I rubbed the tracheotomy scar, as if I needed the comfort of it to ground me in reality. "I thought the doctor was lying. I was sure Spence had suffered, lying there beside me on that filthy toilet floor while the dew settled over us and I was too weak, or too knocked out, to try to help him. While the men who killed him went toddling off to laugh about their exploits. I had the whole scenario worked out in my head."

Chris's words were gentle when he said, "There was nothing you could have done for him. I have no idea what your attackers did afterward, but I can tell you unequivocally that your husband did not suffer from his wounds. He was rendered unconscious with the very first blow of the metal rod." Chris reached over and laid a comforting hand atop my forearm. His touch was cool from the glass of Coke he'd been drinking from. "That little bit of knowledge should give you at least a smidgeon of relief, Tyler. Spence didn't suffer. Not for a second."

I could only stare at his hand as his words assuaged a fear I had held since the moment I woke from the coma. It was true, then, what the doctor said. Spence had not suffered.

Thank God.

I eased my arm out from under his touch. I'm not sure why. "Did you find anything when you worked the crime scene? Fingerprints? Anything at all?"

He shrugged. "Not much. No prints, or I should say, too many prints. Impossible to analyze. At some time or other, everybody in San Diego must have wended their way into that bathroom to take a piss. But we did find the murder weapon. And shoe prints in blood. Boot prints to be exact. Probably from the boots that kicked you in the chest and maybe even broke your fingers."

"Motorcycle boots with chains," I said.

He nodded. "I know, Tyler. I remember everything you told us."

"Of course. I'm sorry."

"Let's get back to business," Chris said, his voice still kind but with an earnest edge to it now, as if it was time to get back on track. He opened the book of mug shots and positioned it in front of me on the coffee table.

"Take your time, Tyler. Study each face you see. I know there are certain things we're looking for. The ugly fat guy with the round face and the mole on his cheek. The skinny guy with the wispy moustache. But don't hunt for those traits alone. Open your mind to each photograph you see. The brain's a funny piece of equipment. You never know what might trigger a memory. You might even get a glimpse of the third man, the one you haven't spoken of. The one you thought you didn't see at all."

"All right," I said, weary already and certain it would do no good, but determined to go through the motions. For the detective's sake, at least.

The book was heavy, and there were three more leather-bound books just like it waiting for my attention. "So these are all the criminals in San Diego?" I asked, running my fingers over the faces on the first page.

Chris shrugged. "Sorry. No. Only the ones dumb enough to have priors."

"Priors?"

"Prior arrests."

"Oh."

So with no hope at all that this was going to lead anywhere, I turned to the album in front of me and tried to focus on the faces I saw there.

An hour later, those faces were all running together. I rubbed my eyes as I closed the last book. The detective reached over and took the book from me, adding it to the stack of others on the floor.

"Maybe it was too soon to try this. You only got home from the hospital today." He gathered up all the dinner trash and carried it into the kitchen, where I heard him stuff it in the wastebasket. He came back and snagged his jacket from the back of the couch.

He looked down at me still sitting on the sofa in front of him. "Don't look so downcast," he said. "Like I told you before, the investigation is just beginning. You should go to bed and try to get some sleep." He plucked a business card from his shirt pocket and scribbled something on the back of it before dropping it on the table in front of me. "If you need to talk, call me. Anytime. My home number is on the back. I'm not a very good sleeper anyway."

He gave me a soft pat on the shoulder and headed for the door, once again juggling the photo albums, this time with his jacket wadded up in a ball on top of the stack. Awkwardly pulling the door open, he turned back just before stepping out into the night. "And don't worry, Tyler. We'll find the ones who did this. I promise."

With that, he turned away, and pulled the door closed behind him. Instantly, my grief buried me again.

CHAPTER FOUR
ANGER

AFTER AN almost sleepless night, I found myself wandering through the house in the darkness before dawn, mindlessly seeking something I couldn't name—something I wasn't sure I wanted to find at all. Afraid of the shadows, I left lights on in my wake as I studied the pictures on the walls, peered into every closet, listened closely for every sound I thought I might have heard coming from a direction I couldn't clearly identify.

As I passed a window that looked out on the backyard, I imagined all sorts of creatures lurking in the darkness, staring in at me, watching my every move. I immediately retraced my steps through the house, closing every curtain behind me, blocking out the night. Blocking out the eyes.

I shivered in my boxer shorts, the only thing I was wearing. Looking down, I could still see the bruised outline of the boot on my chest where the fat fuck had kicked me. The bruise only hurt if I pressed my fingers into it. So I did. Just to convince myself I was still alive. I gasped as I dug my fingers into my flesh and the pain tore through me.

My skin felt clammy to the touch, and I realized I had broken into a cold sweat. Once again, I stood in front of the walk-in closet in the master bedroom and stared at Spence's clothes hanging there. The clothes he would never wear again. A wall of grief slammed into me with such force I swayed, almost losing my balance. Biting back a torrent of bile, I swallowed hard, then rushed to the bathroom and stumbled to my knees in front of the commode. I hugged it, heaving my guts out, and when I was good and empty, I felt a little better. At the sink, I splashed water on my face and brushed my teeth. Toweling the cold sweat from my body, I wrapped myself in

Spence's blue terry robe to take away the chill and recommenced my endless wandering through the empty house.

I stood in the living room, staring at the furniture, the rugs, the book I had been reading before my life went to hell. It still lay facedown, splayed wide on the end table by my favorite chair, where I had laid it almost a month ago. Oddly, I couldn't remember a thing about it—not the storyline, nothing. On the coffee table, Chris's business card caught my eye, and I picked it up to see what he had scribbled on the back. *Call me anytime*, he had written. Twice he had underlined the word *anytime*. And then he had jotted down his home number. I flipped the card over and read the words on the front. *Detective Christian Martin—San Diego Police Department—Homicide Division*. Then a number, an e-mail, and a fax. A small imprint of the seal of San Diego decorated the corner of the card.

This was the man who was investigating my case, I told myself. This was the man who had been appointed to bring Spence's killers to justice. Did I trust him to do that? I wasn't sure. He was a nice enough guy, but he couldn't be much over thirty, so how experienced could he be? And even if he was experienced, I wasn't sure if *anyone* was up to the task. There were too many ways it could all go wrong. Too little evidence. Too few witnesses. Too much hatred and anger for me to ever feel satisfied no matter what the outcome turned out to be.

I dropped the card on the table and tugged Spence's robe a little tighter around myself, fighting back another chill. A siren wailed somewhere in the distance, and I held my breath until I was sure the sound was moving away, not drawing closer.

Looking down, I stared at my empty ring finger. It was a funny thing. The ring that had been stolen had only sat on that finger for an hour or less, but even so, my finger now seemed naked without it. I stroked my knuckle, remembering how it had felt when Spence slipped the ring on my hand. I remembered the shimmering flare of the diamond, the warm glow of the lapis lazuli and the gold as they reflected the moonlight on that last night Spence and I walked the neighborhood streets together.

I moved to the bedroom, opened the drawer to the nightstand on Spence's side of the bed, and retrieved the velvet box the rings had come in. Opening it, I found a slip of stiff paper inside, neatly folded, like a notecard on a bouquet of flowers. Inside the folded paper I read the words, *I love you. Spence.*

I sat on the edge of the bed and stared at the card, at Spence's neat handwriting. He hadn't shown me the card when he gave me the rings. Perhaps he forgot. I realized these were the last words I would ever hear from the man I had married, the man I had sworn to love forever.

And the man who had loved me. Till death us did part.

I carefully tucked the card back inside the velvet box and lovingly slipped the box back into the nightstand drawer. I stretched out on Spence's side of the bed, with Spence's pillow under my head. I closed my eyes and, much to my own surprise, drifted off to sleep. And with sleep came a dream.

In my dream, we made love again, Spence and I. Afterward, the rings were still on our fingers when we nestled together in that gentle afterglow of passion lovers enjoy. The words he had written on the little card inside the velvet box became the very same words I whispered into his ear as we held each other close—as I listened to our heartbeats slow and my fevered, trembling body grew calm in his arms.

"I love you, Spence," I said, my lips against his ear.

With a smile and a *shush*, he pulled me closer. And in the dream, we slept.

THE DOORBELL woke me midmorning. I stumbled to the door and found an arrangement of flowers on the stoop. The delivery guy was already gone. As I reached through the door to lift them from the porch, a chill shot through me. It was the same fear I had felt when I left the house the day before to climb into the cab.

What the hell was wrong with me? Had I become agoraphobic after what happened to Spence and me? Had I turned into a coward? Afraid to step outside my own door, afraid to leave the safety of my own house? Afraid to interact with the fucking world like a normal human being?

I forced myself to stand on the porch for a moment, looking over the rail, clutching the bouquet of flowers to my chest with my one good arm. With my pulse hammering in my head, I saw my neighbors going about their lives—kids hustling off to school, their parents driving off to work. A lost dog, as frightened as I was, ran along the sidewalk and disappeared around the corner. Poor thing. The stray dog reminded me of Franklin, and my pulse pounded harder.

I quickly ducked back through my front door, set the flowers on the floor, and with trembling hands, flipped the deadbolt, locking myself in. And more importantly, locking the world out.

When my phone rang, I almost flew out of my skin. Closing my eyes to calm the fear, I stepped to the phone and reluctantly lifted the receiver.

"Tyler? It's Joey at work. I was so sorry to hear what happened to you, buddy. If there's anything I can do, you let me know, okay? Anything at all."

I squeezed my eyes shut. Joey. One of my assistant bookkeepers. The one who wanted my job more than all the others. "Uh, thanks, Joey. Everything is under control. I'll be back to work one of these days, I guess. I don't know when."

Joey was always so damned enthusiastic about everything. Sneaky people usually are. "Sure, buddy. We'll hold down the fort until you get back. Mrs. Margolis in the head office arranged to send you flowers. Everybody here signed the card. You should get them pretty soon."

I stared at the arrangement of flowers still sitting on the floor by the front door where I'd left them. "Oh," I said. "Tell her thanks. They just came. I have to go now, Joey, the doctor is here."

It was the first thing that popped into my head. Fuck him. He'd never know I lied.

"Sure, Tyler. You take care. Everybody's worried about you. Sorry about—well, you know."

"Yeah," I breathed. "I know. Good-bye, Joey." And I replaced the phone on the cradle.

I had no sooner hung up the phone than it rang again. This time I let voice mail pick it up. The call was from Mrs. Margolis herself. The Chairwoman of the Board. My boss. "Tyler, everyone here is so sorry about what happened. Our thoughts are with you, dear. You take all the time you need to get well, and don't worry about your job. You know we can't get along without you. Well, not permanently, I mean. Once again, we're all very sorry about what happened, Tyler. Get well soon." And the call was ended.

I immediately switched off the answering machine to prevent any other calls from getting through. Then I scooped the detective's card off the coffee table, and laying the card next to the phone so I could read it and dial at the same time with my one good hand, I punched in the numbers.

Christian Martin answered on the second ring. The fury in my voice was uncontrollable. I couldn't rein it in. "How did he look, Detective? Spence. When you saw him at the morgue. How did he look?"

There was static on the line for a good five seconds before the detective answered.

"Tyler, why are you asking me this? Are you all right? Did you sleep?"

I backhanded a tear from my cheek. "I just want to know how he looked, Detective. He was my lover, my husband. I have a right to know what his killer did to him."

I heard a sigh. "Call me Chris. Please. And if you're determined to know these things, then I'll get you a copy of the medical examiner's report. But I really wish you wouldn't. Nothing good can come of it, Tyler. You've been hurt enough. You don't need to dig at the wound any more."

I felt the phone shake against my ear. My hand was trembling. "Thank you," I said. "I'll wait for the report." And I hung up the phone.

A moment later, I turned off the ringer.

TWICE IN the next few days, I tried to leave the house, but my fear held me back. When the food began to run out, I had groceries delivered. With my phone turned off, I knew people would begin to worry. So deciding a preemptive strike was needed, I phoned Janie and told her I was fine and simply needed to be alone. I phoned her home number at a time when I knew she would be teaching so I wouldn't have to speak to her.

I called Christian Martin to ask if any progress had been made on the case, but the answer was always the same. "It's going to take some time, Tyler. Be patient. Let us work the clues. In the meantime, call me anytime you want. Even if it's just to talk. Even if it's just not to be alone."

The kindness in his words always surprised me. My anger at hearing them always surprised me too. And even with the impatience and the frustration and the anger, I found myself feeling sorry for the man. He wanted to help me. I know he did. But when he asked for my patience, he was asking for something I didn't possess. If he had asked for hatred, I could have sent him boxes.

After several days, I stopped calling even the detective. It was just another way I cut myself off from the world. And now that I felt entirely on my own, I had more time to wonder about the fear I felt when I thought of leaving the house even for a moment. I hadn't been off the porch since the day I went to the cemetery.

As my body slowly healed and my remaining bruises faded, my fear of the outside grew. When the gardener came knocking for payment, I slipped him a check through the mail slot in the front door. I continued to have groceries delivered, paid over the phone with a credit card.

When my first week at home ended and the second week began, I knew I would have to find a way around the fear. I had an appointment with the doctor to remove the cast on my arm. It had been on almost six weeks. I could wiggle my fingers now through the end of the plaster cast with only a minimum of discomfort. I was healed. It was time to get the damn thing off.

On the day of my appointment, I phoned the doctor's office and told his nurse I had gone to another doctor to remove the cast. I told her everything was fine, and I was sorry for canceling so late. I'm not sure the nurse believed me, but she didn't have much opportunity to do anything about it since I ended the call before she could refer me to the doc.

As soon as I hung up the phone, I drew a hot bath and sank into the water, cast and all. With a pair of scissors, I dug into the slowly softening plaster until the water was milky around me. Finally, I was able to tear the cast apart with my fingers. And when it fell away completely, I breathed a long-drawn-out sigh of relief.

My arm looked pale and wrinkled from its sojourn beneath the cast, smaller than the other arm somehow. But when I flexed my wrist and fingers, everything worked without much pain. I stood in the milky bathwater and showered off the bits of plaster from my body before climbing from the tub. After drying off, I spent the next ten minutes cleaning the bathtub and throwing the soggy remains of the cast into the trash. I spread lotion on my arm to ease the itching, flaking skin, and once again wrapped in a bathrobe, my own this time, I stood at the kitchen sink, sipping a beer.

Sympathy and get-well cards were still coming in daily, but I immediately dropped them in the trash. I had made the mistake of opening one sympathy card. That was enough. The kind words had made me feel worse than I already felt. I refused to put myself through that again. Still, it was the fear that bothered me most. It was with me every second of every day. But at night it was infinitely worse. Inside the house I refused to let nighttime encroach at all. The drapes remained closed, and the lights remained on twenty-four hours a day. I felt helpless. Unprotected. I checked the locks on the doors and windows repeatedly.

At the beginning of my third week at home, it was my anger that finally convinced me to face up to my fear. My anger—and the medical examiner's report that came in the mail.

I opened the official-looking envelope with the San Diego County insignia in the upper left corner and pulled out two sheets of paper. One was a note from Detective Martin. The note simply said, *The forms you requested may not be removed from the Medical Examiner's office. What I am enclosing here is a recap of the coroner's final report. Chris.*

The other sheet of paper was on official stationery with the same county insignia at the top. Below the insignia were the words Coroner's Report: Case # 46G99, and the date. The date was two days after Spence's death.

Scanning the sheet, I realized immediately that what I was reading was simply a summation of the coroner's findings. It did not explain how the coroner arrived at his conclusions, only that he had. Obviously this paper was intended for police and legal personnel who perhaps had limited knowledge of medicine and forensic science. Still, the form held enough information to make me sorry I had requested to see it thirty seconds after I started reading. Detective Martin had been right all along. I was better off not knowing the truth.

Two sentences in and my vision was already blurred by tears. I snatched words and phrases from the paper like a toad snagging flies from the air.

...Spencer Allen Chang—Age 30—Chinese-American adult male.

...photographed before autopsy both clothed and nude.

...subject's weight 169 pounds 8 ounces—length of body 6 feet 1 inch—dark hair—brown eyes—no scars, tattoos, moles, or other identifying markers.

...prior to assault, subject appears to have been healthy—no indication of drugs in system—no needle marks. No sign of anal penetration, rape, or sexual assault.

...subject identified by sister. Name: Jane Marie Chang.
...blunt force trauma resulting in death, three consecutive blows to the head, each blow causing brain damage, cranial fracturing, and catastrophic blood loss. Any one of the three blows would have proven fatal—subject immediately incapacitated—death followed in a matter of seconds.

...murder weapon found at scene of crime—iron bar 2 feet 5 inches long, circumference 3 inches, weight of weapon 2 pounds 12 ounces—iron bar matches the wounds on the skull. No prints....

…no prints, no prints, no prints. The words kept tearing through my head like mocking laughter.

Furious, I scraped the curtains aside and stared out the living-room window, letting sunshine into the house for the first time in days. The ME's report lay crumpled in my fist.

He's gone. He's really gone. And they'll never catch the fuckers who did it. Never.

I sat by the window until hunger drove me into the kitchen. I ate a bologna sandwich. Chips. Whatever I could find I didn't have to cook.

With my hunger fed, anger finally drove me from the house. Fear be damned.

I threw on some clothes and grabbed my car keys from the dresser where they had been lying since before the night Spence died. Had it really been six weeks? Was that possible?

I stepped into the garage with my car keys in hand, their comforting, familiar jangle like an echo of the past, promising freedom, promising—revenge.

The agoraphobic terror I had been subjected to since my release from the hospital was gone. Just like that. The words on the medical examiner's report had stripped it away like bark from a tree.

Tapping the garage door opener clipped to my visor, I blinked back the sunlight streaming through as the door slid open. The car purred around me like an old friend. Or a war buddy. With a grim smile, I pulled out onto the street and headed west.

I PARKED and stared out over the lawns from the interior of the car.

Doggie Park was busy. With wry amusement, I realized I had no idea what day of the week it was, but judging by all the happy dogs and happy dog owners scattered around, it must be a weekend. I took a deep breath and eased myself from the car.

The day was warm. The sun felt good on the back of my neck. I stared off into the distance at the public bathroom where everything had happened. There was no crime scene tape up, but after all this time, why would there be? Still, it angered me to think Spence's life had been so cruelly stolen from him and now there was absolutely nothing left to show for it. It was almost as if his loss—and mine—didn't matter at all. Our suffering had all been just a teeny hiccup in the universe. Didn't mean shit.

Already seething with anger, that anger I now knew so well, I climbed the fence by the entry gate and sat on the top rail, just as Spence and I had done on that last night. Gazing out over the park, I tried to at least wipe the fury from my face. No sense scaring the crap out of all the poor, innocent schmoes walking their fucking dogs. Still, I suppose something in my demeanor separated me from everyone there. No one approached. No one nodded a "good day" to me as they strode through the gate, heading in or heading home, their dogs back on their leashes, already thinking about dinner, about work, about life.

My wrist and fingers ached, and I looked down at them. My injured arm still looked paler and smaller than the other one. When I returned home, maybe I would start exercising to get some strength back in that arm. Squeezing a tennis ball might help. Or light weights. Anything to get the blood moving and alleviate the pain and weakness of the healing bones.

Hearing the barking and the laughter and the hum of jovial voices around me, I began to feel a little better about being there. The moment I climbed down from the fence and stepped onto the lawn to approach the bathroom, my sensibilities changed. Fury once again settled in. And fear too. That old nemesis made a return appearance, waving all its flags and ringing all its bells. But I ignored it. Or tried to.

I had to see. I had to see where it all happened.

Ten feet away from the doorway to the men's room, I could already smell the rank odor of stale piss and disinfectant. The offset entryway had no real door. Just an opening. One simply walked into the dim interior, did one's business, hopefully flushed and washed one's hands, then walked back out again.

Unless, of course, one was waylaid in the process by evildoers, as old George W. used to call the bad guys. As Spence and I had been waylaid.

The interior was empty, the floor wet with piss, the stench almost overpowering. I stared down at the green concrete floor where I had lain, in and out of consciousness, as Spence lay dead beside me, his blood seeping into a growing pool around him. I remembered the sticky feel of his cooling blood on my fingertips that night. My broken fingertips. I remembered the laughter of the three men, the whimpering of Franklin, the ring of the metal bar on the concrete wall, the flash of light tearing through the darkness from the cigarette lighter, held aloft in a fat brown hand.

I remembered the boot striking my chest, but I had no recollection of the injury done to my hand. Was it the same boot that stomped my hand, fracturing my fingers and wrist? Nor did I remember the paramedics carrying me away—no recollection of how long I had lain here before they did.

Nor did I know how long Spence had lain in his clotting, thickening blood while the police worked the crime scene. I never thought to ask Detective Martin that question, but somehow it seemed very important. It seemed like it should have been the *first* question I asked. The very first.

I did not remember the coroner's van backing up to the bathroom door. Did not remember Spence's stiffening body being peeled from the filth he was lying in and zipped into a black vinyl body bag like so much garbage being hauled out to the curb. How could I? I would have been long gone by then. Taken to be treated, to be *cured*, while Spence remained behind, alone and still. And dead.

I tried to block it all from my mind—what I remembered and what I only imagined.

Still hearing happy barks and laughter outside, I stood in the middle of that public bathroom and wondered what to do next. Now that my fear was dead, now that my anger was more alive than ever, just what the hell was I supposed to *do*?

It seemed odd that my vision was clear, that no tears had come to blur it. My eyes were even adjusting to the dim light. I saw chips in the concrete wall and remembered the attacker striking the wall with the metal rod, remembered the ring of it, remembered the sting of the concrete chip the strike dislodged cutting into my cheek.

And moments later the fat man with the horrific mole on his face—or was it the skinny man with the moustache?—or perhaps it was the third man, the man I couldn't remember at all—

—whichever one it was, he found a better use for the weapon in his hand and turned it on Spence. I closed my eyes, recalling the sound of that first strike. The almost orgasmic sigh Spence made when his life suddenly seeped away. I also remembered the sound of the second and third blows, when Spence made no sound at all. He was already gone by then, I now knew. Already dead. Already lost to me.

I stood in the darkness of that reeking toilet and flexed my fingers against the pain of their healing. Then I clenched my fists so tightly my fingernails cut into the palms of my hands. The pain felt good. It felt necessary. Once more I felt the stickiness of blood against my fingertips. This time it was my own blood. I squeezed tighter, and my fingernails cut deeper into my palm. The pain made me smile.

Still amazed that no tears had dampened my eyes, I turned to the bar of sunlight spilling through the doorway. A shadow fell on the filthy floor. A man walked in, a terrier bouncing at his feet. He had his hand over his eyes, as if trying to adjust to the sudden darkness. I stepped out of his way as he moved toward the urinal in the back.

I strode out into the sunlight and closed my eyes, letting the clean air wash over me, through me. Again the sun felt good on my face. The light felt comforting as seen through the darkness of my closed eyelids.

I opened my eyes and without looking back, headed for the car.

Hatred and rage and loneliness walked with me every step of the way.

Halfway there, a drop of blood slid from my fingertip and spattered the grass at my feet. The moment I saw it fall, I knew what I had to do.

CHAPTER FIVE
GUN

THE STOREFRONT was comprised of stainless steel and glass. It looked high tech and sterile. When I pulled open the door to step inside, an electronic chime rang out, heralding my entrance. The inside was just as polished as the outside, with every inch of the place covered in chrome and gleaming glass and sparkling white floor tiles. It was blindingly lit, like an operating room.

The air was heavy with the scent of gun oil.

To my surprise the clerk behind the counter was a woman. Her hair had been bleached to within an inch of its life, and her skin was the color of almonds. She looked like she slept every night of her life in a tanning bed. The heavily applied pink lipstick she wore clashed with her skin tone and drew my eyes immediately to her mouth—which was gaily smiling.

If any of her inventory had ever killed anybody, she didn't seem to much give a shit.

"How can I help you?" she asked. I caught a flash of leeriness in her gaze as she eyed me up and down, as if she knew she was simply going through the motions. *No sale here*, her posture seemed to say.

"I'm looking for a gun."

Her smile widened, patently false, showing tobacco-stained teeth and a pink wad of gum. "I figured. What sort of gun'd you have in mind?"

"Handgun."

She spread her arms wide to highlight the display case she stood behind. I looked down and saw the cabinet was filled with handguns. The display case stretched from one end of the store to the other. There must have been hundreds of guns in it.

I let my eyes range over the massive selection, hoping I looked like I knew what I was doing, but I'm pretty sure she knew I didn't.

"So how complicated is it?" I asked.

She cocked her head to the side, watching me. "How complicated is what? Shooting, buying, or just looking?"

"Buying."

Her smile faltered and her eyes glazed over as she started rattling off her well-rehearsed spiel. Her gum popped between sentences.

"Gotta be eighteen years old. Looks like you got that one covered. Gotta be an American citizen. Looks like you might have that one covered too. No felony convictions. No history of mental illness. Gotta have at least one hand and one finger to pull the trigger with. That's about it."

I felt a surge of hope. Maybe this wouldn't be so bad after all. I waggled my fingers at her, jokingly showing her I had plenty of digits, at least. I ignored the stab of pain from the fingers that were still healing when I did it. "That's it? That's all I have to do to buy a gun?"

She grinned. "To buy a gun, yes. To assume ownership of the gun and walk out the door with it, there's a few more steps to the process."

"Like what?"

Her gum popped, and her eyes glazed over again. "You have to fill out the PFEC. And before you ask, that's the Personal Firearms Eligibility Check, which outlines all the steps I told you about before. Costs twenty bucks. Requires a thumbprint and a notary's stamp."

"That doesn't sound so bad."

Her eyes were at half-mast as she stared at me. She was obviously bored shitless. I wondered vaguely how many times a day she went through this with inexperienced gun buyers like myself. "Then you have to take a handgun safety test. If there's anything you don't know, for a nominal fee we can help you through that. The next step would be for you to pick out the gun you want, pay for it, and wait ten days for approval."

"Ten days?"

"Yep. That's the law. A lot of whack jobs out there trying to get their hands on a gun. The ten-day waiting period weeds a few of them out. It works under the assumption that if you want to blow your boss away, by the time you wait ten days to get a fucking gun, you won't be pissed off anymore." She gave a nasty chuckle. "Wouldn't work for me. When I get mad, I'm mad forever. Ask my ex."

"Why?" I asked. "Did you shoot him?"

"Not yet. Anyway, that's the drill for buying a handgun if you want to do it right."

I thought about the whole rigmarole she had just outlined. While I was stalling for time, thinking about it, I eyed the guns in the case, trying to act like I actually knew what I was looking at. I don't think she was fooled.

With my pulse hammering inside my head, I asked, "And what if I want to do it wrong?"

Her eyes narrowed, and her pink smile went the way of the dodo, never to be seen again. "Then you'll have to do it somewhere else."

I studied her face for a long moment, finally nodded, spun on my heel, and walked out the door. The electronic chime rang as I left. I didn't see her do it, but I imagined her shaking her head as she watched me go.

I hopped in the car and started driving. I had the yellow pages on the seat beside me, and I went down the list of gun shops that weren't too far away.

The second one was in the Barrio. I figured they might be a little more lax with the rules in the Barrio, seeing as how everybody and his dog already owned a gun there anyway, at least if you went by the headlines in the morning paper.

As I drove I scanned the faces on the sidewalk, unconsciously watching for a fat guy with a mole on his cheek and a skinny dude with a crappy moustache. Or maybe *not* so unconsciously.

The second gun shop was called Espinoza's Firearms and Ammo. It appeared considerably less imposing than the last. There were black bars over a dirty front window and a puddle of urine smack in the middle of the doorway, which I had to hop over to get inside. No electronic chime heralded my entrance here. Just the clatter of a tin bell, which struck the top of the door when I opened it.

The interior was lit only by the sunlight coming through the front window. The fluorescent lights hanging from the ceiling were off. Maybe the proprietor was trying to save on his electric bill.

Two men sat behind the counter, smoking. The whole joint reeked of tobacco. Tobacco and, once again, gun oil. They eyed me suspiciously as I approached. One man stubbed his cigarette out in an overflowing ashtray sitting on the display cabinet in front of him. The other man, a younger Latino in a white T-shirt with his pack of smokes rolled into his shirt sleeve, ducked into the back room, as if it was time to get back to work.

The remaining man leaned his elbows on the display cabinet he stood behind. Like the other establishment, the cabinet was packed with handguns. Only these were a little dustier. On the wall behind the man, rifles and shotguns were on display, but I had eyes only for the guns in the cabinet.

"What can I do for you?" the man asked. He looked to be about fifty. There was a speck of tobacco on the corner of his mouth, and looking at the overflowing ashtray, I realized all the butts were unfiltered. As if he knew what I was thinking, he plucked a speck of tobacco from his tongue with his fingers and wiped it on his shirt. His eyebrows climbed high on his forehead as he waited for me to answer.

"Looking for a gun," I said. "A handgun."

The man was suddenly all joviality and good cheer. I wondered how long that would last. "Certainly, sir. What did you have in mind? Revolver? Pistol? Semi-automatic?" Then he chuckled. "Gatling gun? Rocket launcher? Maybe a fucking nuke?"

I laughed. "Nothing so grand, thanks. Just a small pistol. Something to keep around the house for protection."

"Señor," he said. "If it's protection you want, you should buy a shotgun. Ratchet that thing on a dark night and anybody who's snuck into your house to swipe your silverware will hear it and take off running like a rabbit. You won't even have to worry about loading it. Just the sound of a shotgun cocking will scare the bad guys off."

"I want a handgun."

He shrugged. "Okay, then." He watched me as I eyed the case before him. "See anything you like?"

"I—I'm not sure. I'd like something simple. Something easy to use."

"Have you ever owned a gun before?"

I could feel sweat dribbling down my rib cage. I hoped I didn't look as nervous as I felt.

"No," I said. "This will be my first."

The clerk turned and grabbed an official-looking form from a stack behind him. Then he plucked an ink pen from his shirt pocket and laid them both on the counter in front of me.

"Fill these out please. It's the law, I'm afraid. Once we get the paperwork out of the way, we can decide on the best gun for you. How's that?"

Damn. I stared at the form without touching it. Finally, I raised my eyes and said, "I'll have to do this some other time, I guess."

"Too much paperwork, huh?"

"No, no. It's not that. I just realized how late it is, is all. I have to get back to work."

"Certainly," he said, all joviality now gone from his face. "Well, better run along then."

He was already tugging a cigarette from his shirt pocket as I backed away, thanked him, and headed for the exit.

On the street, I closed my eyes against the pain in my aching hand, then headed for the car half a block away. Before I could get there, I felt a tap on my shoulder. Startled, I whirled around.

It was the other man from the gun shop. The younger one. Not only was his cigarette pack still rolled into his T-shirt sleeve, but he now had another cigarette tucked over his ear like a pencil. He took my arm and tugged me a little farther down the street, past my car.

"Follow me," he said.

I tried to jerk away. "What are you doing?"

He didn't pause but kept on tugging me along. "If you want a gun, follow me. I can arrange it. Do you have cash?"

"Yes. Or I can get it quick enough."

"That's good. Come with me, then."

We walked to the end of the block and turned the corner. Half a block farther, I followed him into an alley. A few paces off the street, he led me down a flight of concrete stairs. He pulled a key from his trouser pocket, unlocked the door, and ushered me in ahead of him.

"Uh, you first," I said, and he grinned but did as I suggested. Once inside he flipped a light switch and pulled the door closed behind us.

I looked around. We appeared to be in some sort of furnace room. There was no one else present. It was dimly lit by a filthy light bulb hanging on a cord from the middle of the ceiling.

The young man dragged a burlap sack from behind an old cast-iron furnace, which looked like it hadn't been lit in a hundred years. He carried the bag to a corner and dumped it on a greasy table. Whatever was inside the bag clattered. It sounded heavy.

He folded back the sides of the sack to show me four pistols. The one he lifted from the bunch was smaller than the others. Short and stubby and black. He laid it in his hand as he rattled off its attributes.

"Smith and Wesson .38 Special Model 60. What we call a five-shot snubby. Got a two-inch barrel, which makes it easy to hide. Carries light at fourteen ounces. It's simple to use. Thought you might appreciate that fact since you don't seem to know what the hell you're doing." He smiled when he said it, and I smiled back.

"You're right," I said, feeling a blush rise to my cheeks. "I don't."

The kid was all business. Friendly and helpful. I wondered if he was still working for the man in the store or if he had taken off on his own entrepreneurial path—the path requiring a shitload less paperwork. He shook bullets from a box, showed me how to load the weapon, indicated where the safety was, then offered it to me to hold.

I took it. My hand was sweaty. The gun felt wrong in my hand. I suspected it always would.

I aimed it at the furnace and looked down the barrel imagining a fat man with a mole on his face standing in front of me.

"Does it kick?" I asked.

"A little, Señor. Just aim a foot and a half lower than where you want the bullet to go. That should take care of it."

Firearms 101, I thought, rolling my eyes. "Loud?" I asked.

He grinned. "Louder than a motherfucker. It doesn't have much punch. Won't stop an elephant. Oughta slow a burglar down pretty good, though. But that's okay. If you don't kill your man with the first shot, the bang will probably scare him to death anyway." Then he chuckled. "Or you."

I laid the pistol on the table, glad to get it out of my hand. "How much?" I asked.

The young man seemed to know he'd made a sale. He didn't appear disappointed by the fact.

"Five hundred. Cash. I'll even throw in some bullets. It ain't much good for anything without bullets. 'Cept maybe pounding tortillas." Comedian.

"I'll take it," I said.

"Thought you would." He wrapped the other guns back in the burlap sack and stashed the bag back behind the old furnace. The gun I had just purchased he unloaded, and he stuffed it and the box of bullets in a grimy backpack that hung on a hook on the wall. He zipped the backpack shut and slung the pack over his shoulder before turning to me.

"I'm assuming you don't have five hundred dollars on your gringo ass."

"No. Sorry."

"Then I'll ride with you in your car to the ATM. Any objections?"

"No," I said.

"Then let's go, Annie Oakley."

I followed the young man back into the sunlit alley. Without wasting time on chitchat, he trailed me to my car.

The guy seemed to know what he was doing. I wondered if I did. I was so worried about that, I wasn't even offended by the Annie Oakley remark. Priorities, I supposed.

AN HOUR later I was back home and the proud owner of a—what the hell was it again? A five-shot snubby? Smith and Wesson .38 caliber something or other? My little Latino friend had even thrown in the grimy backpack, which I dumped on the dining-room table with the gun still inside. After I dumped it, I just stood there looking at it.

A moment later the doorbell rang.

More flowers, I thought. But when I peered through the window, I saw Detective Martin standing on the porch. He was brushing down the front of his jacket as if he remembered what I had said the last time he was here. Again, he looked tired and a little disheveled. I was beginning to think he always did.

He looked up and saw me through the window staring out at him. Since there wasn't enough time to run around the house to try to find a place to hide the gun, I decided to leave the backpack on the dining-room table. Surely he wouldn't go rooting through my stuff and find my illegally purchased firearm. My luck couldn't be that bad.

I pulled open the door, and the detective jumped, looking guilty.

"You weren't supposed to see that," he said.

"See what?" I asked.

He looked down at himself, as sheepish as a five-year-old caught swiping cookies, and resumed dusting himself off. "My cat hair removal system," he said.

I was actually too nervous to grin, but I found myself doing it anyway. "Ah, yes," I said. "Waldo."

He nodded. "Fucking feline."

We stood at the front door staring at each other. When we both finally decided to speak, we did it at the same time.

"Sorry, I—"

"Hope I didn't—"

Then we both shut up again.

To break the tension more than anything else, I stepped aside and swept my hand across the threshold in an exaggerated salami-salami-bologna bow to usher him in.

"Thanks," he mumbled, and stepped through the door. Barely.

"Don't stop there," I smiled. "Keep going."

So he did.

Feeling rebellious, I led him all the way across the living room to the dining-room table and pointed to a chair. "Sit," I said. "Please."

He sat. The greasy backpack with the Smith and Wesson in it lay on the table in front of him. He eyed the filthy bag curiously, then apparently decided to try to ignore it.

He cleared his throat. "I'd like to spend some time with you, Tyler."

This time it was my turn to jump. "I—I don't understand."

Looking horrified, he waved his hands in the air, more like a traffic cop than a homicide detective. Splashes of color stained his cheeks. "No! Good God, no! I mean I want to spend time with you while we retrace your steps the night of the… of the… well, *that* night. I think it might free up some of your repressed memories if we put you back at the scene."

"My memories are repressed?"

His eyes never left mine. "You know what I mean."

I didn't tell him I had returned to the scene already. I didn't show him the cuts I carved in the palms of my hands with my fingernails when I did. I didn't tell him my little trip down memory lane didn't open up any revelations about what took place there in that filthy bathroom on the last night of my happily married life, although it sure as hell freed up a new batch of anger. I also failed to mention that new surge of anger had prompted me to buy what was now tucked away inside the greasy backpack lying on the table in front of him.

And to my sudden horror, I realized he was absently fingering the strap of the backpack while we were talking. What would he do if he knew what was in there? Would he confiscate the weapon? Would he press charges, seeing as how I must have broken several standing gun laws when I bought the damn thing?

Or would he look the other way?

To get him away from the backpack, I said the first thing that came to my mind. "All right. Let's go." I gazed through the dining-room window and saw the sun beginning to set. "It's almost the same time of day," I added, as the memories already began flooding back. Franklin trembling at the door, trying not to explode. Spence beside me, our wedding bands new on our fingers. The taste of Spence's come still on my lips, making me love him all the more.

I shook my head, jarring the memories, even now trying to push them away. It dawned on me this might not be such a bad idea. Maybe I *would* remember something new.

"Do you want to drive to the park?" I asked.

Chris scooted his chair back and stood. "No. Let's walk. Let me just get comfortable."

He stripped off his jacket, hung it on the back of the chair, then pulled his tie away from his neck, tossing it over the jacket. He casually popped a couple of buttons at the throat of his shirt, revealing a scatter of dark chest hair.

"Ready," he said with an easy smile. It was the first time he had ever truly seemed comfortable around me. I couldn't imagine why, but it made me like him even more than I already did. I realized at that moment that Detective Christian Martin was probably a very nice guy, in spite of his line of work.

My heart gave a lurch when he focused on the backpack. "About time you retired this thing, don't you think?" he asked. "It looks like it has more miles on it than I do."

I forced up a chuckle. "You may be right." And to change the subject, I countered his question with one of my own. "Anything to report on my case? Anything new?"

He blinked. "Your case. Uh, no, I'm afraid. Not really."

"Too much time has passed," I said. I could feel the anger setting in once again. Jesus, I couldn't seem to get away from it for two minutes.

Chris clutched my arm. "That's not true, Tyler. It just takes one break. One witness to come forward. One anonymous tip."

I could tell by the expression on his face that my smile wasn't exactly blinding. But then, none of them were these days. "Or one incredible stroke of luck," I added to his list.

"Yes," he said solemnly, studying my face. "A little luck wouldn't hurt either."

CHAPTER SIX
WORDS

TO MY amazement, I found myself enjoying the walk with Chris through the familiar neighborhood streets. He talked lightly of how things had changed in San Diego since he was a boy. I was surprised to learn he had grown up in a house less than six blocks from my own. His parents had sold the home while Chris was in college. They now lived in a retirement village in Del Mar. Detective Martin owned a small condo downtown, close to work.

The shadows were deepening as we approached the gate to Doggie Park. In the distance we could hear the yapping of happy dogs, each and every one of them taking advantage of this small window of opportunity to run leashless and play their little hearts out with others of their ilk before their masters dragged them home. Listening to the dogs brought a smile to my lips and at the same time made my heart ache. I was hit with a sudden rush of loss once again, not for Spence this time, but for Franklin. I wondered where he could be. Had he found a new home? Had he died somewhere alone, wondering all the while what had happened to his two masters? Had he asked himself why they abandoned him the way they did? Did he wonder where they had gone?

Chris must have noticed my change in demeanor. He dragged me to a stop just inside the gate. Gently gripping my shoulders, he turned me toward him and eyed me closely. "Maybe this wasn't such a good idea."

I gave him a brief shake of the head. "No, it's all right. I was just thinking about Franklin. Wondering what... whatever became of him."

Chris nodded as if he understood. And since he was a pet owner, maybe he did. He seemed to also know there was nothing he could say to make me feel better, so he didn't try. He merely turned to face the fence behind us and slapped the top rail, inviting me to join him. "Sit with me," he said.

We perched side by side atop the fence, just as Spence and I had done two months earlier. Just as I had done the other day. Our knees brushed together. Uncomfortable with the contact, I pulled away.

"Sorry," Chris mumbled. I wasn't sure why.

Looking out over the lawns and seeing the red sunset quickly fading to starlight on the horizon, I remembered that fateful night, the things Spence and I had talked about, the unfamiliar weight of the rings on our fingers, the excitement of knowing that because of the rings, our lives were now more intertwined than ever before. Inseparable, that was us, Spence and I. Or so we thought.

Chris waved a hand, encompassing all the people in front of us, most of them standing around chatting with each other while their dogs raced around like lunatics. "Do any of these people look familiar to you? Chances are the people who bring their dogs here do so on a regular basis. Maybe a few of these faces will ring a bell."

I did as the detective asked, never mentioning to him I had been here only a few days ago. I studied the faces in the gloaming, and as I did, the security light high atop the public bathroom blinked on, illuminating the park, casting sharp shadows across the grass. Still, I simply stared out at the people in front of me, offering no comment, dredging up no memories. The silence hung between the detective and me like a layer of fog. Finally he swept it away with a question.

"You look better," he said. "Is your hand healing? How does it feel?"

I gazed down at the hand like someone had just attached it to the end of my arm and I had never really noticed it before. I flexed my fist. "The fingers still ache sometimes. Maybe they always will."

"Hopefully not," he said. "When are you going back to work?"

The question took me by surprise. I realized I hadn't thought about work once—not once—since the day my boss phoned. And Joey. Good old weaselly Joey.

"I guess I'll go back when I can't stay away any longer," I said.

Chris's face softened in understanding. "Makes sense to me." He pointed to a tiny Chihuahua making amorous passes at a German shepherd. We both laughed. "No inferiority complex there," Chris chuckled.

As quickly as his laughter flared up, his face sobered. He turned to me, and said, "It's not good cutting the world out of your life, Tyler. It's not good letting your grief get the better of you." I started to protest, but he raised his hand to shush me. "I've learned a few things about grief in my line of work. I've learned how it can destroy a person. Grief and hatred combined make a deadly cocktail, Tyler. It's a one-two punch that leaves you reeling. Some people never recover from it. I'd hate to see that happen to you."

I looked away—back to the dogs, back to the city skyline on the horizon. Anywhere else but at the sympathy in Chris's face. For some reason his compassion infuriated me.

"I'll be fine," I said, my voice emotionless. Empty. But immediately I was drawn back to Chris's face, Chris's eyes. Something in the empathy I saw there made me wonder things about him I had never considered before. What kind of life did he lead outside of work? What must it be like to see the terrible things he saw day after day, then go home to—who? A cat? One fucking cat? And why was he really seeking me out this way? Was it really to jog my memory? Was that truly the reason he came to see me today? Was that really the purpose behind our getting together?

Or was he simply lonely? And that begged the other question. Was he gay?

"Are you married?" I asked because I didn't have the nerve to ask the other question.

He studied my eyes for a moment, then responded, "No."

"Girlfriend?" I asked.

The slightest smile tweaked the corner of his mouth. "No."

A yip at my feet made me look down. A Pomeranian stood by the fence looking up at me. His fluffy tail was nothing but a blur. One happy dog.

Then a memory kicked in. A memory from that night. The young woman with the Pom. I remembered her words and spoke them out loud. "He's the only male in my life who ever made me happy."

Chris looked bewildered. "What did you say?"

I pointed down at the Pomeranian still standing there looking up at me. "That's what the owner of the Pom said just before she left the park. That night. She told me her dog was the only male who had ever made her happy. Spence told her he knew the feeling, only he was talking about me, not Franklin. Then the woman laughed and said, 'Good night, boys.' As if she understood about us."

Chris's eyes flashed. "*This* dog?" he asked. "The owner of *this* dog?"

"I think so." I lifted my eyes to scan the park. Would I recognize her again if I saw her? I was pretty sure I would. "She was here just before the attack. Maybe she saw something. Maybe she saw the men go into the bathroom. Maybe she can identify them."

My pulse quickened as I scanned the faces around me.

"Do you see her?" Chris asked. "Do you see the woman?"

"No. Maybe she's in the bathroom."

We both jumped when an old lady came out of the shadows behind us and slapped me on the arm, startling me so I almost fell off the fence.

"Suzie likes you," the old woman said with a laugh, scooping the Pom into her arms. She was dressed in overalls and wore a sunbonnet on her head as if she had interrupted her yard work to take the dog out for some exercise.

It was almost fully dark now. The woman gazed out over the park, what could be seen now in the circle of light cast by the security lamp. "Which dog is yours, young man?"

I stared at the woman, disappointed. It was the wrong dog. The wrong person. "I—I don't have a dog," I said.

She giggled. "Then you'd better get one." She snuggled her face into the Pom's coat and lifted her hand to say good-bye. Her eyes were sparkling. Still giggling to herself, she strode through the gate and set off down the street, her little Pomeranian bouncing around at her feet.

"That wasn't her," Chris commented, apparently reading the disappointment in my posture.

"No," I said. "It wasn't her."

"Shit," he said.

I nodded. Shit indeed.

The park was thinning out, only two fat Corgis and an older gentleman remained. Soon, as the darkness deepened, even those three strolled through the gate and disappeared into the city. The two fat Corgis pulled the old man along at the end of their leashes on short stubby legs. Only Chris and I remained behind, sitting atop the fence in the moonlight, staring out over the empty lawn. Night sounds moved in to swallow the silence. A cricket chirped. A night bird chortled in the canyon behind the far fence. A distant siren wailed somewhere down the hillside.

"Maybe I shouldn't have brought you here," Chris said.

"No," I answered. "It's all right. *I'm* all right. It was worth a shot. And, well—it's good to be out of the house with someone. I guess maybe I was getting lonely." Embarrassed by what I had just said, I sneaked a peek in his direction. "Don't take that the wrong way. I just mean—"

I watched a slight smile part his lips in the moonlight. The smile was both gentle and sad. Still, he seemed glad I had said what I said. "I know what you mean, Tyler. You don't have to explain it."

I thought of the gun resting in the backpack on my dining-room table.

"I want to get back at them," I said, once again staring out at the lights of the city in the distance, once again feeling my fingernails dig into the palms of my hands, breaking the scabs that were already there. "I've never felt like this before. So full of hate. So goddamn mad. I'm like a fucking teapot that somebody forgot to take off the stove. Boiling. Boiling." I clenched my jaws shut until my teeth hurt. I'd said enough. I'd said too much, maybe.

I could sense Chris watching me in the darkness, but I was afraid to confront his stare, too ashamed to look his way. I felt tears begin to burn my eyes, and that made me even madder. I had cried more in the past month than I had cried my entire life, and I was getting sick of it. Sick of the futility of it. Sickened by how weak and helpless it made me feel.

When his hand came up to rest against the back of my neck, it was all I needed to push me that one step farther and make the tears finally fall. I brushed them angrily away as his fingers gently massaged my neck. His other hand took mine from atop my leg and held it like a bird, carefully, as if my fingers were made of spun sugar and might snap off at the slightest pressure.

"Tyler, I think it's natural for you to feel this way. My God, how could you *not* be angry after everything that's happened to you? But you can't let your anger destroy you. You still have a life to live. It's entirely up to you how you want to live it. I understand you miss your lover."

I narrowed my eyes and turned to glare at him. "Spence was my husband. He wasn't my lover. He wasn't my boyfriend. He wasn't my trick. He was my husband. And I was his."

Chris nodded, solemn, accepting his mistake. "I know. I'm sorry. I guess I'm just not used to thinking of gay relationships in terms of matrimony. The gay marriage laws are still so new. The words seem, I don't know, *odd*. I even have gay friends who find the wording awkward. Even some of the married ones."

I shrugged, giving him the benefit of the doubt. "I suppose that's true."

Laughter rang out from the trees down the slope beyond the perimeter of the park. It sounded eerie ringing through the darkness. Spooky. A scream tore through the night, followed by a burst of female laughter. Young people fooling around.

Chris stared into the darkness for a moment listening to it, then he turned back to me. His hand was still at the back of my neck, his fingers caressing the hair at my nape. He was being a friend. He was being concerned. Nothing more. But my body was reacting differently. I gave the faintest shudder when his fingertip skidded across my vertebrae. We were so close I could feel his body heat as he sat there next to me. I wondered what he would do if he knew what his touch was doing to me. It had been a long time since I had been touched by a man other than Spence. Hell, it had been a long time since I had been touched by *any* man.

I slid from the fence, and in the process, pulled away from his hand. Purposely. "Maybe we'd better get back."

He dropped to the ground beside me. "If you wish," he said softly, stuffing his hands in his trouser pockets and sucking in a big gulp of night air. He looked up at the emerging stars, and I followed his gaze. The sky was beautiful. The air smelled of ragweed and lilacs. Night birds were singing in the treetops.

I took a step toward the park gate and home, but Chris snagged my sleeve and pulled me to a halt. He waited until my eyes were on him before he spoke.

"I want you to be careful, Tyler. I want you to be careful of yourself. Don't do anything stupid. Promise me. Don't try to take the law into your own hands. Don't make that mistake."

I studied his face, considered his words. It was almost as if he knew about the gun back at the house. But that was silly. There was no way in hell he could know about the gun.

The gun. Why *had* I bought it? What had I hoped to accomplish by purchasing it? Had I really bought it because I was suddenly afraid of the world, or did I have other plans for it? Plans even I hadn't fully decided upon? Was Chris smarter than I thought he was? Had he nailed the truth about my intentions even before I did? And just what the fuck was the purpose of buying a gun unless you intended to use it?

Chris watched me closely. And I watched him right back. Meeting his gaze. To my surprise it was he who looked away first.

And to my even greater surprise, he trailed the back of his hand along my forearm, brushing through the hair there, almost lingering with the touch. Then I watched as he squeezed his eyes shut and pulled his hand away.

"I guess we should go, then," he said softly. I felt a brand-new sense of loss settle into me. But a loss of *what*?

We turned our back on the park, on the settling dew beginning to sparkle the grass, on the coolness of the night breeze stirring the leaves in the trees along the sidewalk leading back through the city streets to my house. I had the strangest sensation that something had happened between Chris and me. Something important. But I couldn't begin to explain what it was.

Occasionally, as we walked the quiet sidewalks, our shoulders brushed, and once the backs of our hands made the slightest contact, gently bumping against each other. While it was the lightest of touches, it was enough to jar me to the core. He felt it too. I know he did.

I cast surreptitious glances at him when I thought he wouldn't notice, and his face was somber. He watched his feet as we walked. He had stuffed his hands in his pockets. His shoulders were hunched inward.

"I appreciate everything you're doing, you know," I said. "Please don't think I'm ungrateful."

He shook his head. "No. Of course not. I understand this is hard for you, Tyler. How could it not be? You've lost—everything."

"Thank you," I said, staring down at my hand, once again eyeing my ring finger in the light of the streetlamp we were walking under, wondering where my ring was now—on whose finger it was resting. Was it on the hand of Spence's killer? The fat man with the mole, maybe? Or the skinny fucker with the crappy moustache? Or maybe it was the other man. The man I didn't remember at all, except for a burst of cruel laughter coming from the shadows of that reeking toilet that night. Who had the ring? And who had *Spence's* ring? Were they both decorating the same murderous hand?

That thought was so crushing I had to shake it away. I felt suddenly weary to the bone.

"I need sleep," I said quietly.

Chris took my arm yet again, steering me along the darkened street like a ninety-year-old relative.

"Yes," he said. "It's getting late. You must be exhausted. I shouldn't have come. I shouldn't have bothered you."

"No," I said. "I'm glad you did."

I was lying, and we both knew it. The silence that settled over us said as much.

"Let me just get you home," he muttered. "Then I'll take off."

I nodded, too disheartened to speak. *My home. My empty home.*

Chris kept his hand on my arm the whole way. There was something about his touch that made me want to cry. Guilt, I guess.

I wondered if Spence could see my guilt. And the wondering broke my heart.

I managed to hold back the tears until I was alone inside my front door. I listened, holding my breath, as Chris's car started up and pulled away.

Once he was gone, I walked through the silent house, switching on lights as I went. I spotted his jacket and tie still draped across my dining room chair. He had forgotten to take them. Then I saw the backpack lying on the table. The backpack with the gun inside.

Again, the question clawed at my mind. *Why did I buy it? What did I intend to do with it?*

I stood in the silent house, my fingers caressing the fabric of Chris's jacket. I slid his tie through my fingers. In my imagination I felt the heat of his body still warming the clothes he had left behind. Lifting the jacket from the chair, I pressed it to my face, inhaling its scent. A surge of desire stuttered through me.

I closed my eyes against the hunger, pushing it away. I draped the detective's coat and tie back over the dining-room chair. Still, my fingers lingered on them until I forced myself to pull away.

And then I reached for the backpack. I unzipped it and tugged the gun free. The pistol felt cold and hard in my hand. Heavy. With my other hand, I tipped the backpack up and a clatter of gleaming bullets spilled out across the mahogany tabletop. I sucked in a deep breath and began slipping the bullets into the gun as the Latino kid had taught me to do.

When the pistol was fully loaded, I flipped the safety to On.

I laid the gun on the dining-room table. Fully loaded now, it frightened me more than I cared to admit. It frightened me because I knew that with just the right amount of courage, with just the right amount of *disconnect*, I could make my anguish disappear in one booming flash of light and sound. I could stop the suffering *now*. I could stop it all.

I hefted the gun once again, measuring its weight, testing the feel of it. I laid my finger over the trigger and extended my arm to aim the gun straight out in front of me. I centered the sights on a painting on the dining-room wall. I applied pressure to the trigger with my uninjured hand, grateful it was the other hand the fucker had stomped on, otherwise the gun would have been useless to me.

Holding my breath, I squeezed the trigger a little harder. My hand began to shake. Then I reached up with my other hand and released the safety. Instead of the painting on the wall, I imagined a face in the gun sights. A fat face. The face was laughing at me. I homed in on the yellow teeth in that evil, laughing mouth. Then I slid the gun a fraction of an inch to the right and aimed the barrel of the gun at the mole on the man's cheek.

I lifted my finger from the trigger and whispered, "Bang."

Carefully, oh so carefully, I slipped the safety back to On and returned the loaded gun to the backpack. Exhausted and heartsick, I walked from the dining room toward the bedroom, stripping my clothes away as I went.

Sleep. I need sleep.

And by closing my eyes to the world, I postponed my fate a while longer.

IF SPENCE'S family had tried to contact me during the ensuing weeks, I knew nothing about it. They didn't come knocking at my door, I knew that much. Even Janie did not reach out to see how I was coping. I was not surprised by Spence's family's reaction to the death of their son. After all, their reactions were not far removed from my own. They had pulled back. If not from the world, as I had, at least from me. And I understood why they had. I was nothing more than a reminder to them of what they had lost. But more importantly, with Spence no longer dragging me into their midst by the simple fact of his loving me, they no longer felt compelled to accept me as one of them. They carried, perhaps even unknown to them, that cool oriental outlook on life that focused on family and little else. I was not family to them. Not anymore. Even when Spence was alive, I was not truly family. It was only Spence's father who was brave enough, and honest enough, to let his indifference toward me show. And now I had pulled away from *them*, they felt no compunctions about letting me go.

And I was glad they had. Without Spence in my life, they meant nothing to me either. They served no earthly purpose other than to remind me of what I no longer possessed. And the same could be said for them. Our common thread, the one that tied us together, was broken.

Spence. He was no longer ours to share. Without him, neither of us needed—or wanted—the other. I let them go without a backward glance.

My in-laws were not the only ties I was about to sever.

Ten weeks to the day after I woke from my coma, I received a letter in the mail from work. The letter was terse and coolly scripted. There was no apology in the words printed there. And strangely enough, the only emotion the words in the letter conjured up in me was to be appreciative of the fact that the message was short and to the point.

The letter bore the letterhead of Mrs. Katherine Margolis, Chairman of the Board, Worldwide Enterprises.

In so many words, Mrs. Margolis was letting me know that since I had chosen to sever all communication with the company, repeatedly not answering phone calls or e-mails, she was taking the only action available to her in releasing me from my position with the firm.

"Good luck, Tyler," Mrs. Margolis ended up. "Everyone here is sorry for your loss and for the road you have chosen to cope with that loss. While we understand it, we still have a company to run. For the interim, Joe Marston will be assuming your duties as Chief Accountant."

And on a more personal note, in a postscript at the bottom, Mrs. Margolis added, "Take care of yourself, Tyler. I wish you nothing but the best. Your friend, Katherine." Below her name there was a cc to Joe Marston, newly promoted Chief Accountant for the company.

I smiled seeing his name there. The little weasel finally got what he had been aching for ever since the day he came to work for me. My job.

And amazingly enough, I didn't care. I wadded the letter in a ball and dropped it in the wastebasket beside my desk.

Twelve hours later, I stepped from the house just as midnight chimed from the old Regulator clock on the living room wall. The filthy backpack was draped over my shoulder.

There was no fear inside me. Not an ounce.

The weight of the gun inside the bag was a comfort. That alone should have scared me to death.

CHAPTER SEVEN
TROLLEY

THE LATE-NIGHT downtown streets were dimmed by a layer of fog rolling in off the bay. The fog billowed across the city, pressing cool against my skin, muting streetlights and deadening sound. I had not dressed for the damp ocean air, and I shivered under my thin shirt. My baseball cap, which I now pulled low over my forehead, kept my head warm, which was one small blessing. The backpack hung from my shoulder, and I hugged it in front of me for warmth. The gun inside felt hard against my stomach. I longed to reach inside and clutch the weapon in my hand but didn't dare. Still, I was comforted knowing it was there within reach if I needed it.

Respectable citizens had long since barred their doors against the fog, but the homeless were out in force, settled in for the night on street corners and tucked into doorways. They were hunched inward for warmth, huddled together singly or in groups, many covered with plastic drop cloths or ratty blankets to ward off the moisture in the air. As I passed, empty eyes peered out at me, but no pleading voices accosted me, no dirty hands reached out to plead for change—a dime, a quarter, a buck. Maybe these people thought I was one of their own. Or maybe they thought I was as crazy or as downtrodden as they were, walking these streets alone in the fog without even a jacket on my back.

The hour was late. Long past midnight. Traffic was light. Occasional sharp sounds split the foggy hush. The crash of a bottle breaking in a gutter. A car horn in the distance. A sharp howl of laughter from some woman, buried under rags, perhaps, cowering behind a rusted shopping cart, making love to her equally homeless partner or sharing a joke as they passed a bottle back and forth to ward off the evening chill or to wash away the bitterness of their wasted existence.

Like I should talk. My existence wasn't exactly riding high at the moment either.

What the hell was I doing out here? Did I honestly think I would run head-on into the three animals who killed Spence and left me for dead? Did I think I would pull my trusty snubnose whatever-the-hell-it-was out of the backpack and blow them away like Dirty Harry?

I shook my head, laughing at myself, and walked on. The damp air was making my injured arm throb like a toothache. Especially the fingers. I wondered if I had removed the cast too soon. Should I have waited? Should I have at least had the common sense to let a doctor do it? The damn thing had been off my arm for three weeks now, and still the pain at times was almost unbearable.

I tucked my aching arm under the backpack, offering it as much protection from the damp as I could, and continued to walk. It felt good to stretch my legs after all the time I had spent cooped up in the house, afraid to go anywhere, afraid to rejoin the world. And before that—the weeks I had spent lying on that hospital bed, unmoving, unknowing. For all intents and purposes as dead on the outside as I felt on the inside.

Roaming the foggy streets, I had time to consider what I should do now that certain aspects of my life had been irreparably altered. I was no longer married. I was out of work. I had absolutely no desire to find another job. And because Spence and I had shown a little common sense and married legally a year earlier, I really didn't *have* to find a job right away.

Being married at the time of my spouse's death meant our finances were already arranged. What was Spence's now became mine. No taxes need be paid. No family members could move in and try to take what was Spence's at the time of his death. And in all fairness, no one in Spence's family had attempted to do such a thing. I had to give them credit for that.

I also gave them credit for having enough sense to know I wanted nothing further to do with them. Not for a while, at least.

And probably never. Even Janie would admit it was better this way. The last thing they needed was for me to be there in their presence every waking moment to remind them of the son and brother they no longer had.

Lost in my thoughts, the sudden roar of a trolley screaming past not more than six inches in front of my face sent my heart shooting into my throat. In my shock, I toppled, almost fell, and a young man standing next to me clutched my shirt collar and yanked me back before I could tumble under the iron wheels of the train rumbling past.

The man was young, black, and amused. I shook him off, then immediately thanked him for saving my life.

He grunted, picked my hat off the sidewalk, plopped it back on my head, and said, "Dumbass. You should watch where you're going," then turned and walked away.

The long line of trolley cars screeched to a stop in front of me. I fumbled in my pants pocket for change, turned to a kiosk beside the tracks, and purchased a ticket. With nothing better to do, I stepped on board the red car, repositioning my hat, readjusting my pride.

The car was empty. Not a soul in sight. I plopped my ass down on the hard plastic seat, and a moment later, the trolley lurched into motion. I didn't know where it was headed until I looked up at the sign by the door leading to the car ahead. I was on the Blue Line. Final destination San Ysidro, the US/Mexico border crossing, and all stops in-between.

What the hell was I doing? Then I thought at least I was out of the fog. At the next stop, or maybe the stop after that, I'd just debark and wait for the return trolley to carry me back to the city. I wondered if I was beginning to show signs of irrational thinking, and the answer to that rhetorical question was so blatantly obvious, I had to grin.

Then a young man stepped through the connecting doors leading from the car ahead.

The minute I saw his eyes, I felt the grin fall from my face.

He wasn't one of the men I sought. At least I didn't think he was. But he was the same *breed* of young man. Latino, obviously raised in poverty, with the same cruel glint in the eyes, the same uncaring take on the world around him. The same anger so obviously boiling inside him you could almost feel the searing heat of it pouring off of him. I could sense his anger in the cocky tilt of his head, the reckless, leonine, predatory way he moved across the trolley floor.

His cold eyes were aimed solely at me. Every ounce of his attention had been trained on me from the very moment the young man stepped through the connecting door from the car ahead.

And why wouldn't it be? After all, he and I were the only people in the car.

The moment I truly realized we were alone, I also realized the danger I was in. The trolley windows were black where they looked out into the night; the lights inside were dim. There were no witnesses, no fellow passengers, and even the driver was five or six cars away. If there was an attendant roaming around checking tickets, he wasn't close enough to be of assistance if things started going wrong.

Which is exactly where things immediately went.

The young man walked directly toward me. He was a handsome kid. Tall. Kind of beefy. He wore cargo shorts and a San Diego Zoo sweatshirt that had seen better days. His legs were strong and hairy, his hands huge. His greasy black hair was pulled back in a ponytail, anchored by a leather string tied snug to the back of his head. He had rings on every finger, even his thumbs. Cheap rings. One was made simply of silver wire bound several times around his finger.

He stopped a few feet from me and stood there, leaning from a passenger strap, staring down at me sitting in the last seat looking back at him. His large hand laid itself across his crotch, and he shifted the weight of his cock beneath the shorts while a teasing grin spread his lips apart, displaying neglected teeth. He explored his yellow teeth with the tip of his tongue as he continued to rub his crotch, which appeared to have grown plumper.

The fucker was getting a hard-on.

"I'm horny," he said with a vicious smirk. "You look like a cocksucker to me. Maybe you can solve my little problem."

I slouched comfortably into my seat and stared right back at him. "So it's little, is it?"

His vicious smirk turned into a nasty leer. He took a step closer and released his crotch to grab two hand straps, one in each hand. He sort of hung there in front of me, hemming me in, swaying with the motion of the trolley car thrumming over the rails. "What did you say, *pendejo?*"

I clutched the backpack a little closer to my chest, continuing to stare up into his face. I spoke a little louder, as if purposely making up for the fact that the man in front of me was either deaf or dense. "I asked you if you had a little bitty dick. You seemed to be worried about it."

He blinked, then cast his eyes around the empty car as if trying to come to grips with the fact that I wasn't afraid of him. Dropping his eyes back to me, he cocked his head to the side, struggling to figure me out.

For the first time, his attention seemed to focus on the backpack in my lap.

"What's in the bag, bitch?" he asked.

But before I could answer, his hand shot out like a rattlesnake, and his strong fingers clamped themselves around my throat. I gasped for air, and he smiled to finally see a flash of fear on my face.

But I wasn't *all* fear. I still had enough anger to go around.

When he worked his thumb into the corner of my mouth, I clamped down on it with my teeth, and at the same time, my foot made contact with his balls. His eyes popped open wide, and he released my throat.

His face grew the color of adobe bricks, and he gasped for a breath of air after my unexpected kick in the nuts. The next thing I knew, he had fished a switchblade out of his trouser pocket, and flicking it open with a tap of his thumb, he pushed the blade against my cheek hard enough to draw blood.

I froze.

"What's the matter," he asked, still seething and looking a little green around the edges after having my size twelve Reeboks buried in his testicles. "Lose your sense of humor?"

I didn't answer. I continued to hug the backpack against my chest with one arm. The other hand, unbeknownst to my attacker, was in the bag. I could feel the teeth of the zipper touching each side of my arm. Inside, the gun was cold metal in my grasp. My finger was on the trigger. The barrel pointed directly at Santa Anna, or whoever the hell he thought he was. If he was expecting another Alamo, he was in for a rude awakening.

For the first time since Spence's death, my anger was totally out of control, and I knew it. I didn't fear this clown at all, and I think the clown was beginning to realize that fact. I had to admit he looked a little nonplussed about it too. I guess he wasn't used to having his powers of intimidation fall short of the intended reactions from his prey.

"Still want that blow job?" I asked, and the knife dug deeper into my cheek. I could feel a rivulet of blood flow down my neck until it was lost somewhere beneath my shirt collar.

His smile came back by degrees. The bulge in his trousers grew more noticeable.

Still holding the knife to my face, he reached down with his other hand, steadying himself against the movement of the train by pressing his hip to the seat in front of me. His grin widened to display his less-than-appetizing teeth as he slid his zipper down and pulled out his dick.

I have to admit it wasn't a bad specimen. Half-erect. Fat. Uncut. He shifted his ass around in his pants to free it all the way, then clutched my chin with the same hand he had released his dick with to pull me toward him.

The trolley car suddenly swayed sharply as another trolley, headed in the opposite direction, brushed by us on the adjoining tracks, rocking the train with an explosion of sound and light. A whistle screamed somewhere outside.

My tormentor pulled his foreskin back, exposing a bulbous cockhead speckled with filth. I was assailed by the stench of unwashed flesh. For the first time in my life, I fully understood how the term *cheesedick* made its way into the lexicon. This fool's unwashed cock, fully erect now, looked like it had been dipped in parmesan cheese.

I glowered up at his leering face, almost stunned by the smell. "The next time you go out looking for a blow job, you might want to introduce your dick to some soap and water first. It's called personal hygiene. Ever hear of it?"

Anger sparked his eyes. "You can wash it for me, funny man. Use your tongue."

I exhaled a tiny burst of air. It was almost a laugh. "You'd have to kill me first. In fact you'd have to kill me *twice* before I'd stick that filthy thing in my mouth."

He grinned broadly. "Then I guess that's what I'll do."

And just as he thrust his hips forward to press the head of his reeking cock to my lips, I pulled away and pushed my back into the seat to gain some distance. The moment I did, I took a firmer grip on the gun inside the bag.

He smiled down at me, his eyes afire with hate, and maybe lust as well. His voice was a sibilant snarl. "No blow job? Then I'm going to cut your fucking throat."

"I don't think so," I said and pulled the trigger.

Even muffled by the backpack, the sound of the gunshot was jarring.

A tiny red flower burst into bloom just above the young man's Adam's apple. He assumed a surprised expression, as well he should have. Toppling backward, he fell as stiff as a falling oak tree. A tiny wisp of smoke issued from the hole in the top of the backpack.

The gun no longer felt cool in my hand, but warm. I released it from my grip, extracted my hand from the bag, and calmly slid the zipper closed to seal the gun inside.

The young man lay unmoving at my feet, eyes open, mouth ajar. There was almost no blood. The .38 caliber slug must have been lodged somewhere inside his noggin, not having enough force to punch its way through his thick skull after traveling through his neck, his tongue, the roof of his mouth, and then whatever brains the guy might have had, which probably wasn't much or he would have washed his dick once in a while.

The trolley car swayed again, and the rumble of the wheels softened. The train was slowing down.

I stood and moved toward the door, stepping over the silent Latino as I crossed the car. His filthy dick, flaccid now, was still poking through his fly, and I felt sorry for the autopsy guy who would have to examine the damn thing. I held my hand to my cheek to staunch the blood still flowing down my neck from the cut on my cheek. There was no pain. I was too excited to feel pain.

With a jerk, the trolley bumped to a stop, the door slid open, and I stepped out into the dark. I didn't know where the hell I was, but it didn't matter. I could always catch a cab home. It didn't seem advisable to be taking any more trolley rides tonight.

With no one on the landing to step inside the car and find the dead body I had left behind, I breathed a sigh of relief and walked quickly, but not too quickly, away from the tracks, my baseball cap pulled low across my face in case there were any hidden security cameras. I jogged down a flight of stairs and found myself in the business district of San Ysidro. Suddenly I knew where I was.

Walking six blocks to the main drag, I hailed the first taxi I spotted.

As I rode home, the Somalian driver, attuned to the night shift, apparently, hummed a tuneless song to keep himself awake. I looked down at my hands as the passing streetlights strobed through the taxi window.

My hands did not shake. There was not a tremor in them.

I studied my hands all the way home, amazed by their steadiness. Where was the fear? Where was the adrenaline? Why wasn't I freaking out?

I caught a glimpse of myself in the driver's rearview mirror. My face was as calm as my hands. No smile twisted my lips, but there was no fear on my face either. I wiped the continuing seep of blood from my cheek with my shirt cuff and tucked my hand back inside the backpack. The pistol was still warm. Once again, with the gun in my hand, I felt safe.

With that reassuring metal heat pressed comfortingly into the palm of my hand, I leaned my head back and closed my eyes.

I thought of Detective Martin the rest of the way home. The dead man on the floor of the trolley barely rippled my memory.

It took me a few miles to realize the driver was humming the theme song to *Leave it to Beaver*.

I remembered back over some of the episodes. Beaver's mom was a hoot. Always dressed to the nines. Didn't she ever just strip herself down to nothing, throw her tits in the air, and ride Ward's boner like a proper slut? I would have. Ward was hot.

I smiled in the darkness as the miles rolled away beneath me.

By the time I arrived home, the gun was once again cool to the touch.

THE NEXT evening, the murder of the man on the Blue Line to San Ysidro warranted only a begrudging thirty-second mention on the local news. Not only did he have outstanding warrants for burglary and assault, he was also undocumented, HIV-positive, and proclaimed a person of interest in a series of rapes in the North County in which two women had been unlucky enough to contract the disease. Had he been tried and found guilty, the dead man on the trolley floor would also have been charged with two counts of attempted murder.

So basically I saved the creep from a lifetime behind bars where he would have no doubt infected half the inmates around him, not to mention all the innocent victims he might have raped before he ever got there.

While there were reportedly few clues to his murderer's identity—nothing but the caliber of the gun used and a grainy security tape of a medium-sized man with a baseball cap pulled low over his face and a backpack on his shoulder—the police also seemed less than committed to expending untold man-hours in their search for the killer's whereabouts. The unspoken attitude seemed to be that the man who took out Hector Gutierrez, lowlife extraordinaire, had done the city a service. Why not leave the guy alone and chase down the criminals that matter? At least that's what I hoped the cops were thinking. And as little else was reported about the crime in the coming days, I began to think that was indeed the police's attitude.

For my part, all I could do was try to forget about it. Or at least that was what I *told* myself I was doing. While I began to feel twinges of guilt over what I'd done, it certainly wasn't enough guilt to put me in a blubbering fetal position. The guy truly was a first-rate scumbag, after all. He might have had nothing to do with Spence's death, but he had most certainly hurt other people. He deserved what he got. He had also tried his sexual shenanigans on me, not to mention cutting me with his fucking knife. Surely, in a pinch, I would be able to plead self-defense. Although it might be a little harder to explain why I was carrying on my person an illegal and unregistered firearm.

The biggest worry I had about the episode was the cut on my cheek. While I knew it was probably a million-to-one shot against the virus being transferred from the creep's blade, I still made a visit to a random doctor and had an AIDS test done. If the guy let his cock get as filthy as he did without cleaning it, God knows what was on the end of that knife. A day later the test results came back negative.

And life went on.

To prove to myself I wasn't completely heartless (and brainless), I decided to put a halt to my foray into vigilantism and retire from the field of battle. In other words, I took the backpack holding the loaded gun down to the basement and stuffed it in the crawlspace behind the furnace. Not because I thought the police wouldn't find it there if they came looking, but because I knew it would be harder for me to access on the spur of the moment in case I took it into my head to go hunting again. I wasn't stupid. I knew I had lucked out. If the police learned I was the one responsible for the trolley death, they would most certainly nail my ass to the wall. And it would be no less than I deserved.

So I put the gun away. And in doing that, I tried to put the memory of what I had done away as well. But still, I felt only the faintest twinges of guilt over what had happened. And perhaps that worried me most of all.

A few days later, Detective Martin came to my door in the middle of the morning. I had just stepped out of the shower and was still in my bathrobe.

The detective had finally been to see a barber, and the barber had almost scalped him. His near buzz cut left his face more angular than it had looked with a full head of hair—and more handsome. His honey brown eyes were big and bright in his narrow face, the long lashes surrounding them even more pronounced. His proud straight nose jutted out from his face, hovering over lush lips and a strong chin with just the hint of a dimple in it. As always, his jawline was smudged with the beginnings of a five o'clock shadow. Apparently, Detective Martin was one of those unfortunate people who need to shave twice a day.

But that haircut!

He saw my amused look the moment I opened the door. Blushing a deep crimson, he ran his hand over what used to be a full head of hair, and said, "I know. My cousin did it. She's in beauty school."

I couldn't help myself. "Still a freshman, I take it?"

Chris glowered and reached under his jacket. "Don't make me shoot you."

I laughed and ushered him inside.

He seemed amazed to see me laugh. He scoped me out from head to toe as I stood there in front of him, still dripping from the shower. He scoped me out so thoroughly, I felt a need to pull the bathrobe a bit tighter around my waist, which caused him to blush again.

Suddenly I knew I didn't have to ask. I was pretty sure the question I had entertained about Chris's sexual orientation had just been answered. Detective Christian Martin was as gay as I was. But his next words knocked that realization right out of my head.

"We have a suspect, Tyler. I want you to come downtown to see if you can pick him out of a lineup."

I was speechless for all of five seconds. "If you have a suspect, why can't I just see him? Why do we need a lineup?"

"If you ID him, it carries more weight in court if you pull him from a lineup. We're not sure this is one of your attackers, mind you. But he's a scumbag, he has no alibi for the day you were attacked, and his physical description matches yours, to a point."

"The fat guy?" I asked. My anger was returning in a rush. For the first time in days I felt cold drops of sweat skidding down my rib cage. My pulse was pounding in my head. Even my injured hand began to ache as if I had plunged it into a bucket of ice water. "Is that the one? Did you find the fat guy with the mole?"

Again, Chris scraped his hand through what little hair his cousin had left on his head. He looked uncomfortable. "I don't want to tell you any more. I want you to attend the lineup with no preconceived ideas. It's SOP, Tyler. We always do it this way."

"SOP?"

"Yeah. Standard operating procedure."

"I know what SOP means." I took a deep, shuddering breath. "Well, good then," I said. "Let me go get dressed."

He nodded. I felt his eyes on me as I left the room. Because I was feeling rebellious, and because I was furious once again about Spence's death, I let the bathrobe fall from my back just as I stepped through the door to the hall, giving Chris a glimpse of my naked back and ass. I wasn't sure why I did it. I just did. I did not turn to see the detective's reaction, nor did I hear him make a sound when I did what I did. I simply left the room and stepped naked into my bedroom to dress.

I had slipped on nothing but a blue dress shirt when I heard a noise behind me and turned to see Chris leaning in the doorway watching me. With my cock flopping around beneath the tail of my shirt I turned to face him, still feeling rebellious. And maybe even a little turned on.

"You cut yourself," he said, tapping his own cheek to indicate where my injury was. "You okay?"

I groped for a lie to explain what the man on the trolley had done to me. I groped a little too long.

Chris's eyes narrowed as he watched me. "You're about to lie. Why would you think you have to do that, Tyler? I'm not accusing you of anything. I just wondered how you cut yourself."

"How did you know I was about to lie?"

"I'm a homicide detective. I get lied to all the time. After a while you start seeing it coming before the perp ever opens his mouth."

My heart stuttered in my chest. "Is that what I am? A perp?"

That seemed to take him aback. "No. Of course not. Oh, never mind. If you don't want to tell me how you did it, don't tell me."

He made no move to leave the room. His eyes were on my body again. At least I imagined they were. I finished dressing without once turning my back to him. If he wanted to watch, I was determined to let him watch. And I still wasn't sure why. At least that's what I told myself.

As I was tying my shoes, I finally dredged up a lie to go with the cut on my cheek. If he chose not to believe it, that wasn't my fault.

"I got drunk the other night and fell off the back porch. That's how I cut my cheek. I was embarrassed to tell you the truth, so I guess my hesitation was what made you think I was going to lie." I chuckled. "Which I guess I really was about to do before you caught me at it."

I studied his face to gauge his reaction. He appeared satisfied. All he did was cluck his tongue and say, "You have to be careful. Drinking yourself into oblivion isn't going to solve anything."

"Neither is falling on my head," I joked.

And to my relief, he smiled. "No, neither is that."

He insisted on driving me downtown in his unmarked car. When I started to climb into the backseat, he laughed and motioned for me to sit up front. "Jeez, Tyler. You're not under arrest. Sit up front like a human."

The car was a mess. Coke cans and sandwich wrappers littered the floor. He had to scrape up a mountain of paperwork off the passenger seat and toss it in the back before I could sit down. He drove with a lead foot. His long legs sprawled wide and his big competent hands maneuvered the steering wheel with graceful ease. I found myself watching him, not unlike he had been watching me back at the house.

He glanced at himself in the rearview mirror. "Fucking haircut," he muttered.

"Actually, Detective, it looks pretty good. You're a handsome guy without all that hair flopping around on top your head."

"Thanks, but I *liked* all that hair flopping around on top my head," he grumped.

I smiled. "Sorry I spoke."

He gave me a glance, then apparently decided to get back to business. "Don't worry about the suspect being able to see you. You'll be behind a two-way mirror. He'll know you're out there, but all he'll see will be his own reflection."

"Do you really think it's him?" I asked. "Spence's... killer?"

Chris looked uncomfortable at that. "No. Probably not. But it's a shot. And just to warn you, I'll probably be arranging a few more of these lineups for you to attend. It's the only way to get your input on IDing a suspect since our mug shots didn't give us any leads."

I twisted toward him as far as my seatbelt would allow. "I appreciate your diligence, Chris. I do. And I know you must be working other cases at the same time."

He shrugged. "It's always that way. Usually on any given day, I have four or five open cases I'm working on. It's the same for everybody in homicide." He turned his eyes to me. "That's not to say that I can't give the proper time to your case, Tyler. I hope you know that."

I nodded. "I know." Then the words were out of my mouth before I could stop them. "I saw on the news about the guy being gunned down on the trolley. Is that one of your cases?"

He shook his head. "No. And thank God it isn't. The guy was such a ratfuck piece of shit I think I might find it a little hard to dredge up a good work ethic trying to find his killer. As far as I'm concerned, the shooter did us all a favor."

I didn't answer. All I could do was hope the detective who *did* get the case felt the same way.

We pulled into the downtown station on Fifteenth Street a few minutes later. Chris parked in the back and led me into the building through a door off the parking lot. We took an elevator to the fourth floor.

He excused himself after ushering me into a tiny room with a table and two chairs. The room was painted a horrific pea green, and a large mirror dominated one wall. There was no one else in the room. Immediately after I arrived, a stenographer walked in with a pad of paper and a small tape recorder, which she set up on the table and plugged into an outlet in the floor. She ignored me until she had everything to her satisfaction, then she cast me a friendly smile and sat in one of the chairs, arranging her notepad in front of her.

"Detective Martin will be back in a minute."

I nodded. She stared at her nails until the door opened behind us and Chris walked in, accompanied by another man. Chris gave me a reassuring smile before he reached out to the light switch on the wall by the door and flipped it, flooding the room with darkness.

The minute the lights went out, another light went on in an adjoining room, which was exposed through what before had been the mirror but was now simply a window. In the other room, six men stood against a wall. Three of the men looked bored, and I suspected they were cops, just there to fill out the lineup. Two of the men looked arrogant. The last man looked scared.

They were all cut from the same mold. Thin, tall, rangy, and Mexican. Two of the men had moustaches that could best be described as less than lush. One had a full beard. The other three were clean-shaven. It wasn't the fat man Chris thought he had found, but the skinny one. The one with the crappy moustache. The one who had swung the metal rod.

"Take your time," Chris said from the darkness at my side.

One by one, the six men stepped forward, facing the mirror. When they were cued by someone I couldn't see in the other room, they each recited the line they had been prompted to speak.

The first man spoke with almost no inflection at all, obviously reluctant to speak the words. He had a thick Mexican accent. "Enough of this shit. Let's kill these fuckers."

My heart shot into my throat. Not at the voice but at the words. Everything about that night came flooding back. I remembered telling Chris during that first interview in the hospital about what the man had said in that darkened public bathroom—telling him about the words I was hearing now.

After dutifully reciting his lines, the man stepped back into the line, and the second man edged forward, as reluctant as the first. He recited the same words in a high, reedy voice with no accent whatsoever. "Enough of this shit. Let's kill these fuckers."

And one by one, the six men stepped forward and played their part.

When the last man moved backward to stand against the wall, I turned to Chris in the shadows beside me and said in a voice hoarse with emotion, "It's none of them."

Then I stumbled my way through the darkness toward the door, those same eight words ringing in my head. Over and over again.

Enough of this shit. Let's kill these fuckers... kill these fuckers... kill these fuckers.

I found my way out of the building and was standing in the parking lot sucking in fresh air when Chris discovered me. He drove me home in silence. Once during the drive, he reached out to touch my hand. Just a gentle brush of fingertips against my skin. Then he pulled his hand away.

"Thank you," I whispered, and as soon as I did, he placed his hand back over mine and left it there all the way home.

At the house, when I finally slid my hand from underneath his and stepped from the car, he leaned toward the open door and said, "I'm sorry I put you through that, Tyler."

I ducked my head in to peer at him. He looked so earnest and caring, I had a sudden urge to clutch my chest to silence the pounding of my heart.

"I need to think about things," I said softly, and he nodded.

In a voice even softer than mine, he said, "So do I."

I gently closed the car door between us and walked away. He didn't drive off until I stepped onto the porch.

I fumbled with the key, and once I was safely in the house where no one could see me, I pressed my forehead to the inside of the front door and closed my eyes.

Spence's face filled my mind. And behind his face, peering through the shadowed memory of the only man I had ever loved, I saw Chris's eyes brightly burning.

Watching me.

CHAPTER EIGHT
FRIENDS

I KNEW my friends in the city must have given up on me by now. It was four months since Spence's murder, three months to the day since I came home from the hospital, and I had spoken to almost no one.

To say my life had changed didn't quite cover the realities of it. I had shut myself away from the world completely. I had lost my job. And while the agoraphobia had lessened of late, I still spent my sleepless nights roaming the house and checking the locks.

But all of this paled next to the fact that I had also committed murder. It wasn't a revenge killing for what had happened to Spence. The man on the trolley had had nothing to do with Spence's death. Still, I had lured him to me that night. There was no denying that. Why else had I gone out into the city with a gun? And now, after getting away with murder, or so I sincerely hoped, I found myself continually thinking of the gun stashed in the greasy backpack and stuffed behind the furnace in the basement. I longed to hold it in my hands again. I longed to once more feel the pressure of the trigger beneath my finger.

I ached to take out my anger yet again on the human race for what they had done to Spence—and what they had done to me. For what they had reduced me to—what they had reduced us *both* to.

Yet hate and grief and anger were not the only emotions I was dealing with. They had carried me this far, yes, but suddenly I found myself with another emotion to battle.

Guilt.

Detective Martin—*Chris*—had begun to intrude on my thoughts more and more, and every time he did, I found myself racked with guilt. Funny that I could shoot a man in the throat and not feel a thing, then turn around and find myself consumed with remorse because of the kindness of the detective in charge of Spence's case. And the feelings I was beginning to have for him.

And what about the motives behind the detective's kindness? Did his attentions mean what I thought they meant? And if they did, how did I feel about that? Or more importantly, how would *Spence* feel about that?

Or was it all imagination? Was I reading the guy all wrong? Was it illusion brought about by loneliness? Jesus, just how desperate for attention had I become? Had I pushed away my real friends, only to now be seeking out friendships from strangers when the old ones would have served me better?

And was it really friendship I was talking about here? Or was it more?

A hundred times a day I remembered the feel of Chris's touch on my skin. Cupping the back of my neck atop the fence at the park. Brushing my hand with his fingertips all the way home from the police station after the lineup. Was Christian Martin just a touchy-feely kind of guy? Is that all it was? Was he simply being kind because he was working my case, trying to find my husband's killer? Was this all part and parcel of the cop/victim routine? Was I really anything more than a case number to him after all? Or was I becoming more?

Two weeks later I found a letter in my mailbox. There was no stamp on it. It had been hand-delivered. I almost tossed it in the trash unopened, but the unfamiliar handwriting on the envelope, a spidery scrawl, really, piqued my curiosity. I ripped it open, and before I read the letter, I skimmed to the bottom to read the signature. Only then did I realize the message came from Chris.

His words were brief.

I'm worried about you, Tyler. Since you won't answer your phone, you've forced me to pull this cloak and dagger crap of slipping a letter in your mailbox to get your attention. Meet me tonight at eight o'clock at the bar we passed that night we walked to Doggie Park. Hess's. The one not far from your house. I want to have a drink with you. And hopefully dinner.

If you don't show up by 8:05, I'll come to your
house and arrest your ass.
    I can't believe I'm doing this. Chris.

Doing *what*? I wondered.

I read the letter three times.

I ARRIVED at the bar ten minutes late. I almost didn't go at all, but something pulled me there. Curiosity, maybe. At least that's what I told myself it was.

The bar had been established in a resurrected warehouse only a couple of years earlier, and Hess's was already one of the most popular microbreweries in San Diego. It was another example of gentrification Spence used to love to cite when he bragged about South Park being his favorite section of the city. We had drunk at Hess's often. To reach the bar, the patrons crossed a grated metal walkway above a dozen gigantic stainless-steel brewing vats where Hess's ale was made.

It was early on a Saturday night, but the place was already booming. It was so crowded you could hardly hear yourself think. Well, no, that's not quite true. The minute I stepped inside, I found myself thinking of Spence with an ache that was almost debilitating. Even with all the racket around me, those thoughts were coming in crystal clear. I tried to shake them away as I forced myself across the walkway and studied the faces at the tables ahead, looking for the detective.

I spotted Chris sitting at a small table near the back. The moment I saw him, he raised his hand in greeting, then he lifted his beer to take a sip. His glass, I noticed, was almost empty. His gaze never left me as I wove a path between tables to join him.

As I approached, he stood and pushed the opposite chair out with his foot, waving me into it. He was dressed in tennis shoes, faded blue jeans, and a white T-shirt, giving me a glimpse of just how long and lean his frame really was. I couldn't help but notice he fit into the jeans very nicely.

Seeing me eyeing his clothes, he said, "Sorry. I wear suits every day at work. You'd have to drug me to get me to wear one when I'm off."

"Understandable," I said, trying to dredge up a friendly smile. I had to drag my eyes away from his hairy forearms to do it. While he was thin and rangy, I could see a pair of very attractive biceps peeking out from beneath the sleeves of his tee. His arms were tanned, the sinews in his forearms constantly moving. There was a beauty and an elegant grace to his large hands with their broad pale nails that drew my eyes every time I was with him. Tonight was no exception. He wore no jewelry. Not even a watch.

He settled himself back into his chair. His pose was relaxed, but his eyes were wary. He looked nervous. I got the impression he was trying to hide his nervousness behind a joke. "You're lucky you showed up, Tyler. I was just getting ready to come over to your house and drag you out in handcuffs. I would have, too, but I couldn't bear to leave an unfinished beer behind. This shit's good."

"Handcuffs," I said. "Kinky."

He blushed, then he immediately took another sip of beer, smacked his lips, and gave me a nervous grin. He opened his mouth to say something, then changed his mind and snapped it shut. He had obviously decided to let my comment go.

I stared at his grin while I parked myself in the chair across from him, uncomfortable at first, leery, just like him. What the hell was I doing here? And why were we both making jokes to cover our unease? But more to the point, why was I so surprised that the goofy grin on Chris's face should make him suddenly so appealing? He looked like a different person altogether. I had never seen a smile create such a transformation before. On anybody.

His teeth were small and white and damn near perfect. Even his horrible haircut was lost and forgotten behind the glow of that gleaming smile. Chris waved a hand at a waitress and held up two fingers as he pointed to his glass. He didn't bother to ask if I wanted something different. And of course he was right. It would have been a sacrilege to order anything other than the house brew. Spence always said the same thing.

"I've tried every microbrewery in San Diego at one time or another, Tyler. This is one of my favorites."

He seemed determined to ignore the fact that we were both obviously ill at ease.

I looked around, groping for something to say. "Spence and I used to come here. It was one of his favorite spots too."

Chris scooted forward, trying to hear me over the raucous crowd surrounding us. It was a happy bar. The ambient noise was almost a roar. People were chattering and laughing all over the place. When the waitress came with our beers, Chris dropped a ten on her tray and waved off the change.

In the dim light, I studied Chris's face. He still looked determinedly cheerful, as if he would consent to no grumpiness on my part. No grumpiness and no grief. This was the first time I had seen him when there was no hint of a five o'clock shadow on his face. He must have just shaved. I had the sudden odd urge to reach across the table and see what his bristle-free cheeks felt like. I shifted in my chair, unhappy with myself for even thinking such a thought.

"If he liked this place, then Spence was a bright guy," he said, studying me, thankfully having no clue the direction my mind had suddenly taken me. "The beer here is great."

He took a long pull from his glass, and I followed suit with mine. I guess Chris felt the need to fill in the silences I was leaving in the conversation, which were many. "There are eighty-seven craft breweries in San Diego. Did you know that? San Diego is quickly becoming known as the Craft Beer Capital of America. Look it up, Tyler. Even Wikipedia says so." He laughed. "And I should know. I've left my ass print on damn near every chair and barstool in every brewpub in the city at one time or another."

I shifted in my chair again. Was it because I was thinking about his ass print, and how that ass undoubtedly looked in those faded jeans he was wearing? I was pretty sure that was *exactly* what I was thinking, which didn't make me feel any less guilty. "So," I said. "I guess that means you're either a connoisseur or a fucking drunk."

At that, he barked out a laugh. "Don't be snide, Tyler. *I'm* not the one who fell off the porch."

I laughed at that, and his face brightened. He tapped his cheek. "You still have a scab where you cut yourself, but it looks like it's healing nicely."

It was my turn to blush. I always blush when I'm caught in a lie. Spence used to find that immensely amusing. "Yes. It's fine now. Clumsy of me. Stupid too." *If it had actually happened that would have been true.* I touched the scab with my fingertip, and the second I did I remembered everything that happened on the trolley. Every word spoken. Every threat made by my attacker. The feel of his knife against my skin. The stench of his unwashed cock as he waved it in front of my face. Even the opening of the rose in the man's throat when my bullet tore through it and the exhilaration I felt when I watched it happen. I took a sip of beer, trying to dislodge that last memory. It made me more uncomfortable than I already was, as if the policeman sitting across from me could actually see the images in my head.

Chris eyed me closely, but his eyes were warm, not suspicious. He leaned in so he wouldn't have to yell over the noise in the bar. "How are you doing, Tyler?"

"How are *you* doing?" I countered, not sure why I felt the need to inflict pain, but I did. "Found any suspects yet?"

He blinked at the anger in my voice. His jaw tightened. "I'm sorry. No. But please don't give up on us yet. We're still working the clues. We're still doing the best we can."

I was ashamed of myself for taking my sudden surge of anger out on him, but I couldn't seem to shut myself up. "I'll tell Spence. He'll be thrilled to hear it."

And the moment the words were out of my mouth, I deflated. The anger simply… sloughed away. I felt like an ass. I reached out my hand and clutched Chris's arm. "I'm sorry. I didn't mean that. I—I don't know why the fuck I said it. Please… just… forgive me."

His hand covered mine, holding my fingers in place on his skin. His skin was hot, his arm hair bristly against my palm. I was stunned to feel my cock move in my trousers. A surge of hunger trammeled through me. Hunger for the man across from me. Hunger to have him naked in my bed. In my arms. It had been so long since I had been with Spence, with *anyone*. I was starving for the touch and taste of another man. But still....

I pulled my hand away and he let it go, but I could see the hurt my words had caused him. I could see it in his eyes.

When he spoke, he kept his voice so soft it was barely audible. "Tyler, I can't begin to know what you're going through. I think I can, but maybe, well, maybe I just can't. I see survivors every day. I hear their stories. I try to empathize. I try to help. But every case is different. Sometimes things just don't work out. The clues don't come in. Those are the times I feel the worst. But we aren't at that point with your case yet, Tyler. Please don't think we are. I've not given up. I don't want you to give up either."

I drained my glass and swiveled in my chair to catch the waitress's eye. I emulated Chris and motioned for two more brews. The waitress nodded and hustled off to fetch them.

I turned back to Chris. Before I spoke, I rubbed my face, raked my fingers through my hair, looked everywhere but directly at him, then finally I settled my eyes on his.

I kept my voice gentle. I could see I had already done enough damage to the poor guy. I didn't want to hurt him any more. "Why did you really ask me here, Chris? What is it you want from me?"

The waitress came with our beers. I waved away Chris's offer to pay and took care of it myself. I sucked the cool froth from my glass and focused every ounce of my attention on the man across from me. "Do you do this with all your cases? Or am I special?"

He didn't hesitate. "You're special." And he left it at that. Two simple words.

I watched him, waiting for more. Waiting for an explanation. But none was offered. He simply sat there staring back at me.

And slowly the explanation presented itself without any help from him.

I struggled to find my voice. Finally, I got the words out. "I'm not ready for... anything."

"I'm not asking for anything," he said calmly. "I just thought you needed to get out of the house. And I—well, shit, Tyler, I enjoy being with you. There's nothing wrong with that, is there?"

I stared at him, soaking in his words. "You enjoy being with me."

His cheeks reddened. "Yes."

I considered that. "Isn't this like a conflict of interest? You're working my case. Should we be socializing at all? Doesn't the police department have rules about that sort of thing?"

He rested his elbows on the table and tapped his fingers on the tabletop while he readied his response. I could see his mind working, could see him trying to figure out exactly how to explain it to me. And maybe even to himself.

"You're not one of the bad guys, Tyler. You're a victim. I suppose it's not the smartest thing in the world for me to become friends with you, but it's not like it's illegal or anything. If you were a perp, it would be a different story. But you're not."

The face of the man on the trolley flashed inside my head, but I shoved it back into the shadows where it belonged. I focused on the living face in front of me. The clean lines of Detective Martin's jawline. His eager, bright eyes staring back at me. The long dark lashes surrounding them.

I got my words out with a minimum of fuss. "You're gay, aren't you." It wasn't a question and he didn't treat it as one.

"Yes," he said. "Does that make a difference?"

"Are you involved with anybody?"

He ducked his head and studied my face. His honey eyes were clear and penetrating. I could see the muscles working in his jaw. "I wouldn't be here if I were, Tyler."

"I guess I knew that," I said meekly.

"Good," he said as a small smile softened his mouth. "At least you know that much about me."

We each sipped our beers, me trying to figure out what to say, him waiting to see what it would be. When his foot accidentally bumped mine beneath the table, he quickly pulled it back and muttered, "Sorry."

"Chris," I said. "I'm not ready for anything."

"You said that already, Tyler."

"You say my name a lot."

He ran his hand over his short hair, his long fingers seeming to memorize the unfamiliar terrain of his newly shorn head while he searched for the right words. When he found them, my heart gave a tiny lurch, as if someone had suddenly nudged it toward the center of my body.

"I like saying your name, Tyler. I like the sound of it. I like the way my lips move when I speak it. I like the way your eyes open up a little wider every time you hear it. It's a great name. Why shouldn't I say it?"

His words made me long for happier times. Times with love in them. Times with romance and cooing words spoken gently in the dark. I gazed down at my beer as I tried to fight back another blush. "You're good at this, aren't you?"

He laid his head to the side, watching me. He looked suddenly confused. "Good at what?"

He doesn't know. He honestly doesn't know.

"Never mind," I said.

While I grappled with the way the evening was going, Chris reached across the table and laid his hand over mine. He obviously didn't care what anybody at any of the surrounding tables thought about two guys holding hands, and frankly, neither did I. And in truth, this was San Diego. Very few people *would* care. He did look intensely worried about how *I* would respond to his taking my hand, though, but even that wasn't enough to make him pull away.

"I really am not asking for anything, *Tyler*." We both offered up a tiny smile when he stressed the two syllables of my name for my benefit. "You are going through something I can barely imagine. And I want to help you get through it. And while I'm helping you get through it, I want to get to know you. I want you to get to know me. I like being with you and I hate to say this, but I don't like many people. Just give me a chance. Please. Having another friend isn't going to kill you, is it?"

"I don't want a trick," I said. "I don't want a romance."

Chris jokingly narrowed his eyes. "Did you hear me ask for that?"

"No."

His hand was still on mine, and suddenly we both became aware of it. We each looked down at my hand snuggled inside his. His thumb came out of the clasp and stroked my wrist. A shudder went through my body. A fire lit his eyes as if he knew.

"Tyler," he said. "Let me just get to know you. Let yourself get to know me. It's not a bad thing, having friends, you know. Sometimes when the world really climbs on your back and beats you into the mud, a good friend is the only thing that can get you through it."

His thumb continued to stroke my wrist, his hand still covered mine. My fingers nestled warmly against his palm. The heat of his skin made my cock move again. I fought the urge to close my eyes and enjoy the sensation.

I tore my eyes from our hands and lifted them to Chris's face. "All right," I said. "Friends."

A smile split his face. His teeth flashed in the dim bar light, and he gave my hand a gentle squeeze.

"Great," he said. "So where would you like to have dinner?"

Chapter Nine
Truth

IN THE days that followed, Chris's consideration and dogged persistence continued to touch me. At his prodding, I began to see past my own problems and reconnect with the world a bit. After he convinced me to open up the lines of communication between myself and the outside world—in other words, plug in my goddamn phone—he telephoned often. He spoke of himself, his work, his family, but seldom my case. I knew his lack of progress in finding Spence's killer was torturing him almost as much as it tortured me. He never called late, only during downtimes at work—when he was driving to a crime scene or when he had five slow minutes at his desk, which was seldom.

And I answered his calls. Every one of them. Often I barely spoke. I simply listened. Chris would rattle on and on about whatever he had called about, usually just little things, and when he started to wind down, the phone would go silent while he waited for my response, which often never came at all. When that happened, I would hear him sigh. But he never took me to task over my unresponsiveness. He merely let it go.

His kindness was bottomless. And apparently his patience as well.

While I wasn't giving much back in our journey toward friendship, he never once gave up on me. And to tell the truth, I began to look forward to his calls. There was something about the mellow baritone of his voice, the calm way he worded his thoughts, the unerring sense of goodness he exuded, that seemed to ease my own pain. My own loneliness.

On a night when the memory of Spence's lifeless body lying in the filth on that bathroom floor got to be too much and I had drunk too many beers trying to push those thoughts away, I broke the pattern and instigated a phone call myself. It was late at night. Well after midnight. Chris picked up on the second ring.

"Speak," he said, obviously expecting the call to be business. After all, murderers don't work on the clock. They aren't restricted to an eight to five grind.

I closed my eyes as the mellow timbre of his voice worked its way through me like a drug. As always, it was accompanied by a considerable amount of guilt.

"It's me," I said, already unhappy I had made the call. "Are you asleep?"

If Chris was surprised to hear me on the other end of the line, it didn't register in his voice. "No, Tyler. I'm not asleep. You okay?"

"I didn't wake you?"

"No. And even if you did, it wouldn't matter."

An awkward silence began to drift in, pulling us apart. It was Chris who reached out to bring us back together. To reconnect. "It's good to hear your voice," he said. "I was just thinking about you."

"That's a lie."

In a calm, certain voice, he said, "Actually, no, it isn't."

Softly, I said, "Why? Why were you thinking about me?"

He coughed up a self-deprecating little chuckle. "Well, that's the $64,000 question, isn't it."

I said nothing because I could think of nothing to say. I tried to think back to why I had phoned to begin with. Was it really just to hear his voice? Could it be that simple? And that complicated?

"*Why*?" he asked. "Is that what you asked me, Tyler? Why was I thinking about you?"

"Y-yes," I stammered.

His voice softened. I could sense him settling in with the phone to his ear. I heard the squeak of bedsprings. He was in bed.

"Tyler, I think you know why I was thinking about you. But there's a more important question I'd like answered here."

"What's that?" I asked. I took another sip of beer. I would be hungover tomorrow, but I didn't care. "What's this big important question you want answered?" *Why was I being such a dick?*

The silence from the other end of the line lasted too long. "Well?" I prodded, with a little more civility.

He cleared his throat. "I just wondered if you were thinking about *me*."

I swallowed. The melancholy in his voice disturbed me. I closed my eyes again and remembered the feel of his hand on mine. The feel of his fingers stroking the back of my neck as we sat perched atop the fence at Doggie Park. I remembered the long line of his legs in those faded jeans he wore that night at the bar. The dark hair on his forearms. The buzz cut hair. The clean smell and look of him. His gentle manner. The assured way he did things.

"I guess I was," I said softly. "Is that bad?"

"No, Tyler, it—"

"Does that make me a bad person, Chris? What do you think? Do you think I should be thinking about the detective in charge of finding my husband's killer in that way? Do you?"

His words came out even softer than mine. "What way are we talking about, Tyler? What thoughts are you having?"

I bit back a sob. The sob surprised me. I didn't see it coming. I took another sip of beer to wash it away completely. I prayed to God Chris hadn't heard it.

"Answer me. Please," he whispered. "Tell me the truth."

Spence's face stared back at me from a picture on the end table. I squeezed my eyes shut to block it out.

"I'm sorry," I said. "I—I don't know why I called. I should let you sleep."

"Have you thought about what I said the other night at the bar?"

"Yes. I've thought about it."

"And?"

I began to feel penned in, herded. "Detective—"

He sighed. "Don't call me that. Call me by my name. All right?"

"All right."

"Tyler, tell me what thoughts you're having. Please. I know this is hard for you. It's hard for me too."

"Why is it hard for *you*?" I asked. Again I heard the anger creep into my voice. I didn't mean for it to be there. It just came.

Another silence fell between us. It lasted until he broke it. "You're in my head all the time, Tyler. I think you know that. And when you're there, I feel guilty that I want to take you away from Spence. But Spence is gone. So why should I feel guilty? Is it because it's too early to expect you to… move on? Tyler? Are you there? Please tell me what you're thinking."

I lifted the picture of Spence from the table and held it in my hand as I stared at it. Spence was smiling in the picture. In life he had always been smiling. It was the first thing people noticed about him.

It took a moment for me to find my voice. When I finally did, I could sense Chris hanging onto every word. "It's all wrong for the two of us to be playing this game."

"I'm not playing a game," he said. "Don't ever think I'm playing a game."

"I'm sorry," I said. "I didn't mean—"

I heard a rasping static on the line, and I knew he had brushed the receiver against the stubble on his cheek. I immediately wondered how that stubble would feel against my lips. Again I pushed the thought away.

He didn't let me finish. "Sometimes I think this would be easier if I wasn't in charge of your case. I'm aching to solve this one for you, Tyler. Don't you know that? I've never been invested in a case as much as I'm invested in this one. I've never really had anything to lose before, you know. All my other cases were important, but they didn't touch me personally. I did everything I could to solve them, but I never figured my happiness lay in the outcome."

"Your happiness?"

"Yes. My happiness. Don't make me explain that. Please."

I thought about what he'd said. "You said you'd never had anything to lose before. What is it you think you might lose if you don't solve this case?"

I could imagine him wiping the sleep from his eyes, trying to focus, trying to make me understand. "You, Tyler. I might lose you."

I heard a soft exhalation. Petulant, maybe. Frustrated certainly. "I know you'll never be able to open yourself up to anybody until this case is solved, Tyler. You'd be less of a man than you are if you did. I'm not trying to ride in on a white horse and rescue you. I'm not trying to make you do anything you don't want to do. But I'm also not ready to simply turn my back and pretend I don't have feelings for you. I'm not sure why the feelings are there, but they are. They started that day months ago when they carried you into the ER. You were in such a sorry state that night, Tyler. Something about you pulled at me. I had never in my time as a detective been so touched by a victim of violence as I was when I saw you lying there on that gurney. Bloodied. Unconscious."

I set Spence's picture aside and strode to the living room window, the phone still at my ear, to look out on the darkened street in front of the house. I spotted a coyote walking along the sidewalk as if out for an evening stroll. He looked up when I moved the curtain to peer outside. The beer bottle was cold in my hand.

"Did you ask for my case?" I asked. Somehow it seemed important for me to know the answer to that question.

"No," he said. "It was assigned to me. I wish it hadn't been, Tyler. I wish I could have reached out to you in other ways. But it is what it is. I have to make the best of it."

"So you have a crush on me," I said. I knew the words would hurt him the moment they were uttered. But it was too late to take them back.

To my surprise, he laughed. "We're not in high school, Tyler. Let me just say I'm intrigued by you and leave it at that."

"Intrigued."

"It's as good a word as any."

I let the silence intrude just long enough for me to brace myself for what I was about to say. It was the real reason I had made the phone call. I knew that now. It had just taken me a while to come to grips with the truth—to admit it even to myself.

"What you said, Chris. About me being in your head all the time."

"Yes?" There was a catch in his voice. I could picture him leaning forward, anxious. Waiting for me to either give him hope or toss him to the wolves. His eagerness and dread to hear what I had to say was so intense I could feel it coming through the receiver like… like an actual physical presence. Like white noise. I could sense him frozen in anticipation, his back ramrod straight, waiting for me to decide his fate.

I knew once I said the words there could be no taking them back, but somehow it seemed right to say them. So I did.

"You're in my head, too, Chris. All the time. I've tried to push you away, but you keep coming back."

After a moment of stunned silence, I heard relief in his voice. There was a smile there too. "I'm stubborn that way."

I didn't return the imagined smile. I couldn't. I tried to clarify my confession, maybe even make it a little less than what it had sounded to be. "But you have to understand. These thoughts are tearing me apart. Spence has been gone less than five months. Thinking these thoughts about you is like turning my back on him completely."

Chris spoke slowly. Carefully. Like a man treading on ice. Afraid to fall through. Afraid to plummet into the icy depths below just when he saw the possibility of rescue, of salvation. "I don't want to replace Spence in your heart, Tyler. I just want you to maybe make room for me too. I can move in slowly if that's what you want. I have all the time in the world. I can wait. Don't you see? I've proven that already."

I nodded as if he could see me. "I know. I know you have."

Suddenly there was hope in Chris's voice. More hope than I had ever heard there. "But you do think about me? Is that what you said, Tyler?"

Again I stupidly nodded, as if he could see me. I still stared out into the night. The coyote was gone. The street outside was empty. I pressed the phone to my ear close enough to hear Chris's breathing. A chill of anticipation went through me at the sound of it. A chill of excitement. Was he lying in bed naked? Was his angular body soft and warm? Were his eyes dimmed with sleep? And how would they look if they were dimmed, instead, with passion? Would the honey in them erupt into flame?

That last thought was too much. I shoved it away. "Yes, Chris. That's what I said. But don't ask me to say it again. I don't think I can."

"All right, all right," he breathed into the phone as if placating a child. "Once is enough. At least I know now that I'm really there. In your thoughts. Inside your head. Thank you for that, Tyler."

"I—I have to go now. I need to sleep. So do you, I imagine."

He laughed. "I may never sleep again."

"Good night, Chris."

"Good night, Tyler." His words were soft and muted. A tremor swept through me at the sound of my name on his lips. My eyes opened up a little bit wider, just like he told me they did.

Gently, I disconnected the call.

In the distance, somewhere out in the darkness, far from the house now, down in the canyon, maybe, the coyote gave a plaintive howl. I dropped the curtain to seal out the night and retreated into my thoughts.

For the first time, I admitted to myself I was happy Chris was in there with me. In my head. Maybe even in my heart.

But would Spence ever understand it?

THE NEXT day a call came from the lady in the office at Holy Cross Cemetery to inform me the tombstone was up. She apologized for the delay, assuring me these things take time and she hoped I understood. I immediately brushed aside her apology, and after thanking her, I grabbed my car keys and was out the door. I chewed my lip as I drove, wondering how the stone would look. I tried to block the memory of last night's phone call with Chris. It felt too much like cheating.

As I stepped from the car at the curb closest to Spence's grave, my cell phone buzzed in my pocket. I fished it out and read the display. It was Chris. I stuffed the phone back in my pocket unanswered. Walking across the dew-soaked grass, I approached the grave.

The grass was filling in now, the sod had taken root nicely. Spence's new tombstone stood at the head of the grave. A simple stone. Spence's name, date of birth, and date of death were carved across it in a square of polished marble. The rest of the stone—top, sides, back—was rough and unpolished, the stonecutter's chisel marks still there to see. It was a beautiful marker.

Unlike the person it honored, it would last forever.

Fresh flowers stood in a vase alongside the stone. White lilies. I wondered if Janie had placed them there. I berated myself for not thinking of bringing flowers myself.

The tombstone was cool to the touch, not yet warmed by the rising sun. I wondered if Spence could feel the weight of the stone as he lay beneath it in the ground. Did it comfort him, and did he know I was here? Did he sense my presence nearby as he always had when he was alive? Or was his world simply darkness now? No memories, nothing. Death.

"I'm sorry," I muttered into the morning air. "I'm sorry, Spence."

There was no response. The silence seemed to bury me alive. I felt like I was drowning in the hush. The words might as well have not been said at all. It was as if the wind had carried them off before they could register an impression on any living thing.

I bent, pressed my lips to the cool stone, then turned and walked away. Back in the car, I punched in Chris's number. He answered immediately.

"Good morning, Tyler." I could hear what sounded like a coffee cup clattering on a tabletop. "You okay?"

I stared out over the forest of tombstones. Except for one, they were the stones of strangers. A black phoebe, my favorite bird with his little black tuxedo jacket and white spats, the dark feathers on his head combed back in a sleek pompadour, fluttered onto the hood of my car and preened himself in the morning sun. When I made a tiny movement behind the wheel, he spun his head in my direction before taking off with a startled chirp.

"Can you come over tonight, Chris? I'd like to see you." The words sounded unhurried, casual, and unimportant in my ears. My thudding heart was more representative of the facts. I was not only guilt-ridden, I was scared to death.

"Yes," he said simply. "Thank you, Tyler. I'll be there as soon as I can get away. Probably around seven. Want me to bring dinner?"

"No," I said. "I'll cook."

"Holy shit," he said. "You can cook?"

"We'll see," I said and immediately snapped the phone shut.

With a final glance at the new headstone, standing on the hillside looking lonely and forlorn, not unlike myself, I twisted the key in the ignition. The morning sun had crested the treetops. The day was beginning. It would be a hot one.

"Spence," I whispered into the silent air just to hear his name. As I gathered speed, I rolled the car windows down to let the wind blow away my thoughts.

It only confused them even more.

CHRIS WAS wearing the same clothes he had worn to Hess's a couple of weeks earlier. Faded jeans, a white tee, and tennies. Once again, he was clean-shaven. He smelled of Sea Breeze and Spearmint gum. He must have stopped at his condo long enough to clean up before coming over.

He was almost an hour late. He was already apologizing as he walked in the door. "There must be a convention of shitheels in town. They're knocking each other over like bowling pins. Got a dead drag queen at Chee Chee's Bar and Grill downtown and three dead druggies in a garage in Shelltown. But enough about me," he blithely finished up, his face lit with macabre humor.

His eyes warmed, the honey in them melting to a softer shade of brown. He aimed them at me like a kid wielding his father's shotgun. Chris had no idea how dangerous his eyes were.

"Hi." He smiled.

"Hi," I said back, forcing a returning smile to my face. I pointed to a chair. "Sit."

He tossed his car keys on the coffee table and plopped down on the sofa instead. He patted the seat beside him. "Only if you'll sit with me."

I did as he asked but left plenty of room between us.

He gave me a hurt look, mostly for show, and gazed around the room. "So what'd you cook. It smells great."

"I lied to you," I said. "I'm a terrible cook. I ordered pizza. That's what you smell. It's probably as tough as shoe leather now. It's been sitting on the kitchen counter for over an hour."

He rubbed his hands together. "Great! I love pizza! The tougher the better. Hell, I even had it for lunch."

My face fell. "Oh."

He grinned. "Kidding, Tyler. Relax. You could be serving Alpo for all I care. Cops will eat anything, you know. No discrimination whatsoever. Bunch of animals, really. Did I mention I was sorry I'm late."

"No. You must have forgot."

"I'm sorry I'm late."

I nodded. "Good to know."

"Cops are always late. Socially, I mean. It's just the nature of the beast."

"I'll remember that."

He watched me to see if I was buying his rambling bullshit. Oddly enough I was. It dawned on me suddenly that perhaps he was just as nervous as I was. That little bit of insight gave me a boost. I tried to relax. I smoothed down the front of my shirt and pushed my hair away from my eyes.

Chris studied every move I made with a gentle curiosity. "You're nervous," he said.

"Yeah, well. So are you."

And the moment I said it, a silence settled around us that was a little less awkward than some of the others we had shared.

He looked over at the end table beside the sofa and spotted Spence's picture. It was the same one I had held the night before as we spoke over the phone. I watched Chris closely as he studied Spence's face in the studio snapshot.

Chris's words escaped as if of their own volition, unaided by him at all. "He was beautiful."

I moved closer on the sofa to better see the picture too. When I did, Chris scooted toward me, as if meeting me in the middle. "Yes," I said, near enough now to feel his heat. "Spence was beautiful inside and out. And more than that, he was a good person. They shouldn't have done what they did to him, Chris. He didn't deserve it."

Chris turned to study my face. His hand came out to rest on my thigh. "No," he said, his word as gentle as his touch. "No one deserves the cruelties I see, Tyler. I'm sorry those cruelties found a way to reach you. I really am."

I stared at his hand on my leg. Letting myself go, I slipped his thumb into my fist and held it tight. Again I eyed the photo in Chris's hand. "No one will ever love me as much as Spence did. I'll never know that kind of love again. I think maybe what Spence and I had only comes along once in a lifetime. When I lost it I lost... everything."

Chris twisted his body to face me. His eyes were kind. He carefully placed the picture back on the table. The moment he did, he lifted his hand to lay it to the side of my face.

"That's not true, Tyler. You haven't lost everything. You still have *your* life. You're a good person too, you know. Spence wasn't the only good part of what you two had together. And as for being loved as much by anyone again—how can you say that? There could be somebody out there right now who's aching to worm his way into your heart. He might even be closer than you think."

I looked away. "Chris—"

He didn't let my interruption stop him. "It depends on whether you give this mythical person a chance or not. Don't you think? It depends on whether you *let* love find you again."

I shook my head. "It won't be the same."

"No," he said. "It *won't* be the same. How could it be?" He scooted closer and began to pull me into a hug, but before he did, he gave me a look, as if waiting for a signal it was all right to do so.

I lowered my eyes and allowed his arm to slide around me. Before I could stop myself, I had pressed my face into the softness of his shoulder as his hand cupped the back of my head and his fingers burrowed into my hair. With his other hand still on my leg, he wove his fingers through mine and held me against him. The skin of his neck was red hot against my cheek. The sensation was so electric, I closed my eyes to shut out all other stimuli. When he spoke, his breath flowed warm and sweet across my ear. I could feel his lips moving against my skin.

"It's me, Tyler. I'm that mythical person who wants to worm his way into your heart. You know. Just in case you hadn't figured it out yet."

I smiled against his shirt, and when he felt my smile, he pulled me closer. While his hold on me tightened, his voice grew softer. I could hear the beating of both our hearts behind it, like the gentle drumbeat behind the melody of a song.

He stiffened. It was as if he knew this was his one big chance, and come hell or high water, he was going to let it all out, damn the consequences. I could feel the intensity and truth in every word he whispered.

"I told you last night on the phone, I can wait, Tyler. And I can. Just don't ever think you'll never find anyone again to share your life. Don't ever think that. If you'll let me, I'll prove it to you. I will. When you need me, I'll be there for you. I promise. When you're ready to continue your life and stop feeling alone, I'll help you find your path. You can trust me. Okay?"

I didn't want to ask the question, but I couldn't stop the words from spilling out. "Can I trust you with my heart, Chris? Can I trust you with that?"

He twisted his head just enough to lay his lips to my temple. "Yes," he breathed against my skin. "You can trust me with your heart."

With that he eased me far enough away that he could study my face. Our eyes held for a scatter of heartbeats. "Tell me you understand," he said softly. "Tell me you understand what I'm saying."

My voice sounded strange to my ears. Fractured, breathy, weak. I had never heard myself speak in that voice before. "Yes," I said. "I understand. Th-thank you."

Both of his hands came up to caress my face. His thumbs slid across my lips as if he wanted to actually *feel* the words I had spoken. He leaned forward and kissed the tip of my nose. Then he pulled back, smiling.

"See? No tongues. I'm patient. Just like I said I was."

His eyes sparked with life. Maybe it was for my benefit, maybe it was for his own, but he coughed up a tiny laugh. He let out a whoosh of air like a man who has survived his first skydive. Still happy to be alive and in one piece. Perhaps he had not been prepared to open himself up to me so completely. But he had, and now he seemed glad it was over. Still, his thoughts were more with me than with himself. His next words proved it.

"Do we really understand each other?" he asked softly.

I nodded. "Yes."

He slid the back of his hand along my jawline. Once again he brushed my lips with his thumb.

Before I could stop myself, I reached out to do the same. I hesitantly touched Chris's full lips with my fingertips, then I slid a hand over his closely shaven cheeks. His skin felt like silk. As smooth as warm milk. Closing his eyes for a moment, he leaned into my hand as if enjoying my touch. When he opened his eyes, he smiled.

"Now feed me," he said. "I'm starving."

Later, after setting the table and microwaving the cold pizza to warm it up, I found Chris standing by the living room window, but he wasn't looking out.

He was staring at the baseball cap in his hand. It had been hanging on the hat rack by the door.

He grinned when I entered the room. He pointed to the insignia on the cap. "Mickey Mouse," he said.

I took it from his hand and tossed it back on the hat rack. "I bought it in Disneyland. Spence and I went there last year."

He stared at the hat rack for a moment, before allowing me to lead him into the kitchen.

After dinner, I stepped out onto the porch with him as we said our good nights. He breathed in the night air.

"I smell hibiscus," he said.

I nodded. "Around the corner of the house. And there's another bush in the backyard."

He looked up at the stars overhead and I followed his gaze. The big dipper was right there. I had the oddest sensation I could simply reach out and pluck it from the heavens.

"Chris," I said softly. "I'm still not ready. You know that, don't you?"

"Yes," he said, as softly as I. "But I'll be here when you are."

With that, he reached out to brush his fingers along the inside of my arm, giving me a chill. Then he turned and walked away.

LATER THAN night, I woke with Chris's scent still in my head. I lay naked on the bed, eyes wide, staring blindly into the dark. My mind was a boiling cauldron of memories, impressions. The feel of Chris's hand on my leg. The moist warmth of his lips on my temple. The gentle way his breath stirred my eyelashes. The heat of him. The clean fragrance that roiled off his body. The caring way he spoke and moved and smiled.

The way his voice carried directly into my heart as we sat on the sofa and he whispered his feelings to me—his feelings *for* me.

Alone in my bed, the darkness lay over me like a lover. I could feel it pressing its feverish limbs against me, holding me in place. My hand slid across my chest. I trembled at the sensation of heated skin beneath my fingertips. It had been so long since I let desire take me over I had almost forgotten how it felt. I imagined my hand to be Chris's hand. I brushed my fingertips—*his* fingertips—over the tender skin of my stomach. Then I trailed my hand along my hip until I felt the bristle of hair on my thigh. Would Chris's leg feel like that? Would he tremble as I was trembling now when my hands explored *his* body? Would he react as I was reacting? Would he feel the same hunger, the same need I felt?

Would his cock lie hard against him, against me, moving gently with the rhythm of his thumping heart as mine was? Would I feel the satin heat and iron hardness of it when I slipped it into my hand, as I was doing to myself? Would his knees come off the bed, as mine did, when I skidded my thumb over his urethra, smearing warm drops of desire across the head of his cock like myrrh? Anointing. Causing him to gasp. Causing him to shudder. As I was gasping. As I was shuddering.

I stroked the hardness in my hand, gently at first, my mind still afire with thoughts of Chris. I could feel his hands on me as they came out of the darkness—out of my imagination—to touch, to explore, to learn the feel of me. To discover what I needed, what I liked. To share with me what my body was experiencing. To make love to me just as my mind was making love to him.

His mouth was on me now. I could feel it drawing me in. I could imagine my cock buried in that satin heat. My thoughts were so aflame, the sensations so real, I flung my head to the side to bury my face in my pillow as my balls drew up into my body and the come inside me roiled, begged, *pleaded* to find a way out. The pressure for release was almost unbearable. My breath was a continuing gasp of pleasure and need. My heart a booming thunder inside my chest. Inside my head.

I flung my arm across my face and scraped the hair on my forearm across my lips. I imagined it was Chris's arm. Chris's hair.

My hand pumped my cock more urgently now. Unstoppable. Faster. With long luscious strokes. The hardness I felt in my hand was a wonder even to me.

"*Chris*," I breathed into my skin as my back arched even higher.

And then it happened. At the moment of release, just as my seed began spilling from my body and I cried out with the pleasure of it, I saw Spence's face peering out at me from the darkness beside the bed.

He seemed sad. Sad but understanding. His cool hand cupped my chin as the come flew out of me, splattering my chest, my face, my pillow. He forced me to stare into his eyes as I emptied myself into the night. Then he did as he would have done in life. He bent his head to lick the juices from my body. To taste me. Relish me.

At the first imagined feel of his mouth on my skin, my eyes flew open and I realized—*I was alone.*

I heaved myself from the bed on trembling legs, my come-splattered body still trembling with release. I stood so long staring at the moonlit canyon through the window that my juices began drying atop my skin, so long that my heart ceased to thunder and buck inside me.

I closed my eyes against the night and reached out to take Spence's hand.

"It's time for me to go," I said softly into the shadows, into the memory of Spence before me. "It's time for me to find happiness again. Let me do it, Spence. Let me go."

His fingers slid from my grasp, and when I opened my eyes, he was gone.

CHAPTER TEN
LAPIS LAZULI

IT WAS Saturday night. The Gaslamp district of downtown, just steps from the bay, was host to a bubbling mass of humanity. As they did every night of the week, tourists, locals, and the indigent all came together at the Gaslamp to dance their strange interwoven dance of excess, survival, and need. Most of the time these separate factions simply danced around each other at a safe distance, one never really acknowledging the other. At other times they started bumping heads. The bumping-heads part was the aspect of the Gaslamp—and the world in general—where Chris's particular talents came into play. A lot of murders happen when human heads start bumping together. When they did, it was Chris's job to clean up the mess and assign blame.

Chris had asked me to meet him there for dinner. Afterward he wanted to show me the view from his condo by the water and introduce me to his cat, Waldo. Before the showing and the introducing actually began, we sat at a sidewalk cafe, sipping beers, trying to decide where to eat, and watching a steady stream of humanity stroll by. Chris's foot was snuggled up comfortably next to mine beneath the table, our knees touching. It had been three weeks since I phoned him for the very first time. Not a day had passed since that we hadn't spoken, either in person or on the phone.

I had yet to pull Chris into my bed, nor had he taken me into his, but the day was nearing. We both knew it.

Tonight I longed to make love to him and would undoubtedly have given in to his slightest urging, but Chris was the one being strong. Not me. He had sworn not to pressure me into beginning that new facet of our relationship until I made the first move. That way, he'd said, he would know I was ready. Chris was a smart guy. He knew I had not completely overcome the feeling that I was cheating on Spence. But those feelings of guilt were gradually fading, and I'm sure Chris knew that too. At least I hoped he did.

While there were many things Chris did know about me, there were also a few things he didn't know. He didn't know about the gun stashed behind the furnace in my basement. He didn't know I had once used that gun to commit murder. And he did not know— not really—that I had made my peace with Spence about taking another lover.

He also didn't know I was in love with him. But before I could commit to that fact, there were matters that needed clearing up. Spence's murder, for one. My own act of murder, for another. I knew I would need to come to grips with both crimes before I could totally open my heart to Chris. Before I could open my heart to *anyone*.

The night was balmy. A breeze wafted through the city streets, carrying with it the ocean smells from the bay. Chris's hair was finally growing out. I wondered if he would give his niece a second crack at it when he needed another cut. Hopefully not. Our fingers lay intertwined atop the table, and to an outside observer, we might have appeared to be long-standing lovers. On this night, we had even dressed alike. Jeans, tees, tennies. I was beginning to appreciate Chris's habit of dressing for comfort during those times when he was not at work.

And speaking of work....

"I have another month of freedom," I was saying. I had just given Chris the latest news on the matter of my unemployment, which apparently was not to be a matter of unemployment very much longer. "Mrs. Margolis granted me that much. The bitch."

Chris laughed. "What exactly did she say when you called to tell her you were ready to rejoin the human race and asked for your old job back? You told me you had been replaced."

It was my turn to laugh. "I had been. By Joey Assmunch, my arch nemesis. But it seems Joey's high opinion of himself, coupled with an astonishing lack of productivity, didn't endear him to the boss or to any of the poor sons of bitches who had to work under him.

I don't know why it took the CEO three months to figure out what a twit he is. Anyway, the minute she did figure it out, she knew she wanted me back. Apparently I called at the perfect time." I shook my head in disbelief. "I finally did something right with my life."

Chris slid a little closer to the table so his fingers could cover mine completely. He leaned in, beer in one hand, eyes focused on me alone. It was as if there were no milling crowds around us at all. The world had suddenly been reduced to a bubble containing Chris and me and two steins of craft beer. "And where do I fit into the assessment as to what you've done right and what you've done wrong with your life?" he asked. His mouth twitched into a smile, but there was some serious thinking going on behind those honey brown eyes of his. "Tell me, Mr. Head Accountant. In which color ink are you penciling me in? Black or red? Asset or liability? Am I a profit or a fucking loss all the way around?"

He took a long pull from his beer while he waited for my answer. I realized suddenly his smile had faltered. He was watching me like a cop, looking for a sign that I was about to lie, that I was about to tell him what he wanted to hear even if it wasn't the truth.

He needn't have worried. On this question, there was no lie inside me.

I squeezed his fingers. I offered myself completely to his scrutiny. And while I was offering that, I also offered up the smile he seemed to have lost. "It's because of you that I'm not still hiding in my house and drinking myself into a stupor every night. It's because of you that I don't spend all my time thinking about everything I've lost. Now I think about–"

He stiffened almost imperceptibly. "What, Tyler? What do you think about?"

"You," I said. "I think about you." I wondered if it was time to say what I really felt, to give him what he really needed to hear— maybe what we both finally needed to hear.

"I know you think about me," he said, studying me even more closely. "But that's not what I asked. I asked if—"

"Asset," I vehemently whispered. "*Asset.*" My gaze fell to his hand clenching mine. His hands were so beautiful. Large, strong, tanned. I loved that luscious sweep of dark hair sprinkled over the back of them and the way that hair then melted into the thicker pelt of hair on his wrists, his forearms. The hair stopped at the crook of the elbow. His biceps were paler and smoother than the rest of his arms. I could close my eyes and know exactly how they would feel against my lips—that's how much I had fantasized about them.

When I raised my head to gaze into his eyes again, I found those eyes still boring into mine. He had an odd expression on his face. Odd, sweet, and romantic.

"I want to tell you something, Tyler. Don't let it frighten you, please. Don't let it scare you away."

"Tell me," I said, a little breathless at the way he was looking at me. A sudden hunger filled me. A hunger to hear the words he was about to speak. "Please tell me," I said again.

I didn't have to ask a third time. Clutching my hand tightly, he pulled me toward him until my hand, still in his, lay snug against his chest. I could feel his heartbeat on the skin of my knuckles. I could feel the pulse in his wrist tapping out the rhythm of his life against my own wrist. When he spoke, his voice was soft and urgent and as breathless as mine had been.

"I told you about seeing you for the first time that night the paramedics brought you into the hospital. The night Spence... was killed. I told you how the sight of you tore at me that night." Chris tugged me even closer. "Nothing's changed, Tyler. You still tear at me. If you suddenly decided to step back and pull away, to find another path down which to pursue your life, one that didn't include me, I honestly don't know what I would do. I'm nuts about you, Tyler. And with every new day that passes between us, hell, every *hour*, every fucking *instant*, I'm even more nuts about you." He gazed off into the crowd for a second before turning back to me. There was a jubilation on his face I had never seen there before. He still looked worried, but he looked determined too. And he looked empowered that he had finally dredged up the courage to say what he was saying. "I've been biting back those words long enough, Tyler. Tonight I had to let them out. Please tell me you understand."

"You know I do," I said softly.

He suddenly sat up and glanced around at the other tables. No one was watching us, and he quickly recentered his attention on me. He watched me closely, his eyes wide and eager. I smiled and he smiled a tentative smile back. My breath caught at the beauty of that innocent, hopeful smile.

"I want to meet Waldo," I said. "Take me home." I didn't care about his cat. His cat was the last thing on my mind.

"What about dinner?" he asked softly.

"Fuck dinner," I said.

He immediately groped into his pocket and extracted a fistful of one-dollar bills. He dropped them on the table for a tip and tugged me to my feet.

"Let's get out of here," he said.

We walked hand in hand through the milling throngs of revelers. I don't know what they were reveling about. It was just a Saturday night. Third Saturday of the month. What reason was there to celebrate *that*? People were packed so tightly together it was all they could do to keep their footing, let alone be worried about two guys holding hands as they walked down the street. Still I worried for Chris's sake.

"What if you see someone from the force?" I asked, trying to pull my hand away.

Chris kept a firm grip on my fingers. He wasn't letting me go anywhere. "I've never hidden the fact I'm gay," he said. "Not since I made detective anyway. I was a little more circumspect when I was patrolling the streets, but those days are over."

"How did you get to be a detective so young?" It was a question I had been wanting to ask.

He spat up a chuckle. "The chief of police's daughter was assaulted in her dorm room on campus at San Diego University. I worked the clues on my own time and found the culprit in less than a day. The chief was impressed enough to stick me in homicide, the place where every beat cop wants to end up."

"And you love it," I said with a smile.

He glanced at me as he tugged me through traffic to cross the street. "Does it show?"

I laughed. "Oh, yeah. It shows."

A flash of sadness crossed his face as we passed beneath the light of a theater marquee. "*You* haven't loved it," he said. "I haven't played my part in your drama like you were hoping I would, have I, Tyler? I've failed you from the very beginning."

I had to look away from the torment on his face, but even as I did, I gripped his hand all the tighter. "You said yourself the clues don't always come together. The hatred still burns in me for the people who did what they did to Spence, Chris, but don't ever think that discontent extends to you. I would kill them in a red-hot minute if the opportunity presented itself, but I'd never do anything to hurt you. I hope you know that."

As we walked, Chris sidled closer to me until our shoulders brushed. "Thank you for saying that," he said. "I don't want anything to come between us. Not even my failure as a cop. And I still think we'll nab them sooner or later. They're bound to slip up. Somebody is bound to come forward. Oh, hell, I don't know. *Something's* bound to lead us to them. I still believe that. You've got to believe it too."

"I do," I said. "Don't worry. I do." But did I really? Could it be possible I was beginning to give up on ever finding Spence's killers? It had been five months, after all. If Lady Justice was going to get around to solving this one, she'd better get her law books out of her ass and get on with it.

And it was at that precise moment, with that asinine thought still echoing through my head, that I gazed through the crowd ahead. We were seeking a path through the milling mob of people going this way and that along the sidewalk. The mob was so thick they were even spilling out onto the street to get where they were going. At that moment—at that *precise* moment—*I saw him.* Dead ahead.

"My God," I muttered, stumbling to a halt, dragging Chris to a stop with me.

He stared at me. "What the hell is wrong? You're as pale as a ghost."

I raised my arm and with a trembling hand pointed to the man twenty feet away eating a hot dog. He was wearing a red bandana around his neck, blue jeans with a silver chain hanging at his waist to secure himself to his wallet, and boots with chains dripping off them. The *same* boots that had been visiting me in my dreams for months.

Chris looked to where I was pointing. "It's him," I said, crushing Chris's hand in mine. "The man with the iron bar. He's right there. *Right fucking there!*"

Before the last word was out of my mouth, two things happened. The man in the red bandana glanced up and saw me pointing at him. He flung his hot dog into the street and, with a curse, took off running. At the same moment, Chris took off after him, pushing pedestrians out of his way as he went. As he disappeared in the crowd, I saw him groping at his side as if reaching for his shoulder holster. I heard him scream "Fuck!" when he realized he was unarmed.

When the shock released me and I began to take stock of what was going on, I took off running after Chris. I knew immediately it was hopeless. I was less than a dozen yards into the crowd when I realized he was no longer in sight. Neither of them were. Neither Chris nor the murdering fuck who'd slaughtered Spence.

I ran anyway, as hard as I could run. People cursed me for shoving them out of the way and seemed to take delight in blocking me every step of the way. I stumbled to a stop less than three blocks from where I'd started. I was out of breath and dripping with sweat. People were staring at me as they passed, wondering if I was on drugs, maybe. Or drunk. Or crazy.

I ignored them as best I could and stood at the curb bouncing up and down on my toes, trying to see over the heads around me, trying to get a glimpse of either Chris or the man in the red bandana. It wasn't until five minutes later that I remembered my cell phone. I pulled it from my pocket and punched 8 on my speed dial.

A moment later Chris answered. He was as out of breath as I was. And furious.

He was so angry he was spitting his words. "I'm sorry, baby. The fucker got away! I called dispatch and put out a BOLO. But I doubt they'll spot him. I saw him fling the red bandana away as soon as he knew I was chasing him. He knew it was like hanging a flag on himself. The fucker ran like a rabbit. *Son of a bitch.*"

I pressed the phone to my ear and listened to Chris mutter more curses. Finally, he asked, "Where are you?"

I looked around, trying to pinpoint my location. I had to push my way through the crowd still filing back and forth along the street until I could read a street sign. "Corner of Eighth and K. Where are you?"

Chris was still breathing hard and sputtering angry curses. "I'm in the East Village, by the ballpark. It's right around here that I lost the fucker. Go on home, Tyler. I'm going to keep looking for a while. He may show up again."

"It was him," I said again. "The man with the iron bar. The man who killed Spence." I still couldn't believe I had been so close to him, and still he got away.

Chris shushed me, trying to keep me calm. "I know, baby. I know. And we'll get him. I swear we will. At least now we know he's still in the city. Just go on home, Tyler. I'll call you later."

Defeated, I began retracing my steps back toward my car. "All right," I said. "I'm…." My voice faltered.

"You're what, Tyler? What were you going to say?"

"Nothing," I said. "I'm just sorry about tonight."

"There'll be other nights," he said quietly.

"I know. Good night, Chris."

"Good night."

"And good luck."

"Yeah," he groused as if speaking to himself. "I'm going to need it."

I snapped the phone closed and stuffed it in my pocket. Heartsick, I weaved my way up the crowded sidewalk. Spence's murderer had been right there. *Right there.*

And still, the overriding thought in my head had been to tell Chris I loved him.

Jesus. Were my priorities fucked up, or what?

A FLURRY of gang killings hijacked Chris's spare time for almost two weeks after the foot chase in the Gaslamp. We spoke on the phone, but each time we did, Chris seemed more distant. More… preoccupied. I saw him twice, but each time he only stopped by the house for a quick hello before hurrying back to the streets to work the crimes he had been assigned.

The third time I saw him, he said he would bring some homework with him to the house if I didn't mind. I was so anxious to see him by then, I told him he could bring a corpse with him if he wanted. He laughed at that, but the laugh sounded forced.

He arrived at eight o'clock. When I offered him dinner, he said he had already eaten.

He pulled a videotape from a paper bag and laid it on the coffee table. I sat beside him and picked the tape up to look at it. It was labeled Security Tape—San Ysidro Trolley Station.

My heart did a somersault inside my chest, but I coolly turned my eyes to Chris to find him studying me.

"What?" I asked, all innocence, dredging up a curious smile from somewhere, trying to act calm. Trying to act *normal*.

"Do you know what that is?" he asked, pointing to the tape in my hand.

I read the label again. "Yeah, it's a security tape from the San Ysidro Trolley Station. Says so right here. Is this what you're working on?"

"It's one of the cases I'm working on."

"I thought they didn't give you the trolley shooting. That's what this is, right? A tape of the guy who did the trolley shooting a while back. The scumbag that was murdered on the Blue Line?"

"Yes. I'm giving the investigators a helping hand."

"Why? Don't you have enough on your own plate without taking cases from someone else?"

"That's how the force works, Tyler. We help each other."

I gazed down at the tape in my hand. I'm not sure where I found the courage to say what I said next.

"Would you like me to play it for you? This is your homework, right?"

Chris's eyes narrowed. A lazy smile spread his mouth, but his eyes were wily. There was no smile in them. "Sure, Tyler. Stick it in. We'll watch it together."

And to my surprise, it was just like the night of the shooting. My hands were steady as I slipped the tape into the VCR. While I gathered up the remotes to carry them back to the couch, I asked calmly if Chris would like a beer. He said no.

There was no fear in me. None whatsoever. Had I so distanced myself from what I'd done to the man on the trolley that it no longer registered in me at all?

"You ready?" I asked, and Chris nodded.

I switched on the TV.

I took Chris's hand as the tape came alive on the screen. A tiny clock in the lower left corner displayed the slow passing of seconds until Chris plucked the remote from my hand and hit Fast Forward.

He knew exactly where he was going. As the tape sped ahead, I watched the trolley stop morph from daylight to darkness in a matter of seconds. A few trolley riders raced back and forth across the platform, disappearing into the cars or flying down the stairs to the street below. Trains slid into the frame and just as quickly slid back out again. Chris hit the Play button just at the two-hour-and-twenty-minute mark on the tape, and all activity slowed to a natural rhythm in the space of a second.

Suddenly the San Ysidro Trolley stop was dark and empty. A stream of light poured over the tracks to the left, and in eerie silence, since the tape had no sound, a string of red trolley cars slid into view. Immediately, the doors opened, and from the door closest to the camera, I watched myself step through the trolley door and pull my baseball cap down over my eyes. I adjusted the backpack on my shoulder and slipped down the stairs to the right to disappear into the night. Moments later, the trolley doors closed and the train slid away in the opposite direction from which it had come.

It was the end of the line. The trolley was now moving north. With a conductor's car at both ends, it didn't need to turn around.

Chris hit Pause, then Rewind. We watched the sequence of events a second time. Then a third. After the third and last time, Chris hit Stop and leaned back on the couch. His hand was still in mine. With his other hand, he tossed the remote onto the coffee table.

"Was that the shooter?" I asked.

"We think so."

"You can't see his face," I commented.

"No," he said. "You can't."

"He's wearing my Mickey Mouse hat," I said calmly. "At least it looked like my hat. I guess your killer likes Disneyland too."

Chris nodded. "I wondered if you'd notice that."

"You want a beer?" I asked.

And again he studied my face. "Sure. Why not?"

I ran to fetch it.

He followed me to the kitchen and stood in the doorway to watch as I leaned into the fridge to extract a couple of Buds.

I straightened, twisted the caps off the bottles, placed them side by side on the kitchen table, then turned and walked directly into Chris's arms.

His eyes opened wide in surprise, but at the same time, his arms came up to pull me against him. He bent his head to press his face to my neck, and I spread my hands over his back and tugged him close.

"I've missed you," I said.

His voice was muffled as his lips moved against my neck. "I've missed you too."

"We've hardly seen each other since the night in the Gaslamp."

"I know, Tyler. I'm sorry."

We stood that way for a long moment. He smelled of gentle sweat and weariness. He had had a long day. His heat was so heavenly against me I couldn't bear to think of him pulling away. Before I could stop myself, I pressed my lips to his hair. It was about an inch long, now, and was as soft as down against my mouth.

"Tyler," he said softly. "No matter what motivations you think you might have for doing it, I told you once not to think about taking matters into your own hands. Do you remember?" He traced a finger across the still visible mark from the cut on my cheek. It had healed now, but a thin red scar still remained. Maybe the scar would always be there. I didn't know. Chris's touch was gentle on my face, and I closed my eyes to feel it better.

"Yes," I said. "I remember. Why?"

"No reason. I just…. I just want you to remember you made that promise. I don't want you to forget it."

"I won't," I said. "I'll renew it now if you want." I stepped back just far enough to gaze into Chris's eyes. They were sad, I thought. Sad and leery. "Would you like me to do that? Promise you again?"

He nodded as his hand came up to caress the side of my face. He squeezed his eyes shut and then opened them again, watching me.

"I promise," I said. "From this day forth, nothing like that will ever happen. I swear." *And I mean it,* my voice echoed in my head. *I got away with murder once. At least I think I did. I won't risk it again. Ever. It would mean risking everything. It would mean risking... you.*

Chris couldn't hear my thoughts, thank God, but he had heard my words. He let them hang in the air for a dusting of moments. Then he said, "Thank you."

He slid a thumb across my temple and pushed me gently to arm's length.

"I have news, baby."

Something in the way he spoke the words ripped into me like a knife. I tensed in his arms. "What is it?"

He took a step backward and slipped his hand into the inside pocket of his sport jacket. He pulled out a small glassine bag, the kind cops use on TV shows to carry evidence.

Inside the baggy was a gleaming gold and diamond ring with a streak of lapis lazuli encircling it.

"Good lord." My knees almost buckled. I couldn't believe what I was seeing. I reached out for it, then immediately snatched my hand away as if Chris were holding a snake. "Where did you find it?"

"So this *is* yours," he said softly.

"Yes. It's the ring Spence gave me the night he…. What about the other ring? Spence's ring. The one with a circle of onyx. Did you find it too?"

"No, Tyler. I'm sorry. We only found this one."

"Where? Where did you find it?" I finally gathered enough courage to take the bag from Chris's fingers and pull it open. The ring fell out into my palm, and I carefully slid it over my finger. Just as it had the only other time I slipped it on, the ring fit perfectly.

Tears filled my eyes as I pressed the ring to my lips. When I turned my attention back to Chris, I saw his eyes had misted over too.

"It was hocked," he said. "The pawnbroker reported the ring from our list of stolen items we mail out to hockshops every week. It just came in two days ago. Five months after the crime, the perps finally decided to get some money for it. Maybe they thought we wouldn't be watching as closely now. Who knows what they were thinking. Anyway, you've got your ring back."

I swallowed hard. "Thank you, Chris."

"You're welcome." With a touch as light as feathers, he cupped my chin in his hand and forced my eyes to his. "Remember your promise, Tyler. Don't test me—" He bit back on the final word he was about to speak.

But I knew what he had meant to say. He had meant to say "Don't test me—again."

Apologizing for the wasted beer, he retrieved the videotape from the VCR, dropped it back in the paper bag, and stepped to the front door.

"Kiss me good night," he said from across the room.

I raced across the floor and took him once more into my arms. He pressed his strong hands to the sides of my face and held me firmly as he laid his soft lips over mine. He held the kiss until my hunger for him was whetted. Then he pulled away.

The ring felt odd on my finger. Cold. Impersonal. Heavy. It was a stranger to me now. It felt… wrong.

The man in my arms felt exactly right.

"I love you, Chris," I said. "I want you to know that now."

Again, his eyes opened wide as he let my words wash over him. He clutched the front of his shirt as if stilling his beating heart. "I love you too," he said slowly. "Don't ever think I don't." And stepping away, he walked out into the night, closing the door between us.

I stood in my empty house and wondered if I had lost him forever. Then I thought of the videotape and wondered what else I might have lost.

CHAPTER ELEVEN
LINEUP

CHRIS LET me stew in my own fears for two days, and then in the afternoon of the second day, my phone rang. After a hurried conversation that did nothing to ease my fears, I found myself once again at police headquarters in the butt-ugly pea green room with the ratty table and chairs and the gigantic two-way mirror on the wall. Just like last time, the stenographer followed me in and set up her tape recorder. She then positioned herself at the table with her steno pad in front of her.

When she was settled, she nodded to me. Perhaps she remembered me from the time before. Or perhaps she was just being polite.

I motioned to the paper and pen in front of her. "Low tech," I said.

She smiled and gave a tiny shrug, then focused her attention on the blacked-out mirror on the wall. She looked bored.

We waited in silence until Chris entered the room. I hadn't seen him since the night he brought the security tape to the house. I opened my mouth to say hello, then slapped it shut. He stood before me with a black eye and one ear covered with gauze. The knuckles on his right hand were bruised and scabbed over. He constantly flexed them as if they hurt. On closer inspection, I saw that the white part of his damaged eye was bright red. A blood vessel must have burst. Either that or he had scratched the surface of his eye.

"My God," I muttered.

"Don't worry," he said quickly, his eyes darting to the stenographer, then back to me. "I'm fine. Just a little run-in with one of your perps." Then he backtracked. "At least, I think it was one of your perps. That's what you're here to tell me. Are you ready?"

He reached out and laid his uninjured hand over the light switch. The moment I nodded, letting him know I was ready, he flicked off the overhead light. Immediately afterward, the two-way mirror came alive.

Once again, there were six suspects standing against the wall.

I stepped closer to the mirror, and when I did, Chris approached the mirror with me. Our shoulders touched. He whispered into my ear, "Don't rush, Tyler. We've got all the time in the world."

I could barely hear Chris's words, for the moment the lights went on in the lineup room, my pulse began thundering inside my head. My vision narrowed to a single beam of sight that encompassed absolutely nothing but the man standing second from the left in the lineup.

The fat man. The fat man with the horrific mole on his cheek.

I reached out in the darkness and squeezed Chris's hand. Luckily, I grabbed the uninjured one.

"Wait," he hissed. "Take your time."

The first man in the lineup stepped forward. If I hadn't been so strung out, I would have laughed. He was so obviously a cop he might as well have been wearing a badge.

"Enough of this shit," the man recited tonelessly. "Let's kill these fuckers."

As the first man stepped back to the wall, I heard someone out of my line of vision urge the second man forward. The fat man.

He slouched three steps away from the wall and stood there glaring belligerently into the two-way mirror. His fingers were nervously plucking at his trouser legs. It was the only display of unease he demonstrated, but it didn't matter. Not to me. I had ID'd the fucker the moment the lights went on in the room.

"Say the words," someone said, and the fat man turned his head to glare at the speaker. Then he turned back to the mirror. His hand came up to touch the mole on his cheek, as if for comfort. Only then did I notice scabs on his knuckles and a Band-Aid on his forearm.

I looked at Chris's injuries, then back to the fat man. Chris gazed stoically forward, not giving me any cause to ID the man for any reason other than my own memory.

The fat man had a faint Mexican accent. His eyes were at half-mast all the time he spoke, as if to prove how unmoved he was by the proceedings.

"Enough of this shit," he grumbled. "Let's kill these fuckers." Then he winked at the mirror, an action obviously directed at the person trying to ID him. When he stepped back to the wall, he had a smirk on his face as if he believed he'd won that round.

Before the third man could step forward, I tugged on Chris's sleeve with trembling fingers. "That's the one who held Franklin's leash. I recognize his face. I got a good look at it when he flicked the cigarette lighter."

Chris snapped his fingers at the stenographer seated behind us, but I already heard the tape recorder whirring and the scratching of her pen on paper.

"Try to speak louder, Tyler. We're recording this. And his voice?" Chris prodded. "Do you recognize his voice?"

"No," I said. "The fat man wasn't the one who said those words. I'm not sure which of the other two it was, but it wasn't him. He said something that night, but I don't remember what it was. I—I don't recognize his voice at all. But it's him, dammit. I'll never forget that fucking face."

I was shaking all over, with fury more than anything. Chris gripped my hand more tightly. "Calm down, Tyler. We're not done yet."

He tapped on the mirror, and immediately the third man stepped forward into the light. He recited the words blandly then moved back to the wall as if he did this ten times a day. And who the hell knows? Maybe he did. He was another cop.

It was all I could do to tear my eyes away from the fat man to pay attention to the other suspects. *We've got him. What the hell are we putzing around with these other guys for?*

I contained my impatience until the last man stepped forward. He was obviously Latino. He had a tattoo on the side of his neck of what looked like a dying rose. Tattooed petals fell from the blossom onto his chest. I could see them through his half-open shirt.

"Cute," I mumbled. The man was ugly as sin.

Not only was he ugly, but he was thin and wiry and wore the same belligerent look on his face as the fat man did. Looking more closely, I could see a resemblance between the two. The skinny guy even had a mole, only in the course of all his DNA pulling together in the womb, his mole had slid from his cheek to below his ear. But it was just as grotesque as the one on the fat guy.

Coincidence, I thought. Then number six opened his mouth. Again, his accent was mild. It was the street accent of every Latino criminal in training. Raised in poverty, steeped in hatred, they all spoke the same language, sounded alike. At least to my ears.

Like the fat man, the ugly guy smirked as he recited the words. "Enough of this shit. Let's kill these fuckers."

I leaned forward and pressed my hand to the glass to retain my balance. "It can't be. It can't be."

"What is it, Tyler? Do you recognize the voice?" The skinny Latino stepped back into the line, unaware of the reaction he had caused on the other side of the two-way glass.

"Yes," I breathed, still in shock. "He's the one who said the words that night. He's the one who spurred the other guy to use the metal rod on Spence. He's the one who started it all." I turned to Chris, studying his face in the shadows beside me. "You knew. You knew it was him."

"I suspected," he said, loud enough for the stenographer to hear. I could still hear her jotting down everything we said. "He's the fat man's brother. We arrested them together in a crack house just off the Barrio."

"How did you find them?" I asked, euphoria setting in. Hatred too. Hatred more than anything.

"We tracked a cell phone that made calls to the pawnbroker who bought your ring. It was the fat guy's phone. The little guy was carrying it at the time."

I still couldn't believe it. "You found two of them. Two out of three. You've got 'em."

Chris nodded. "And with your testimony, I'm pretty sure we can keep them. They don't have any other outstanding warrants on them, but that doesn't matter. Now that they're in our custody, we can compare them to the trace elements we found in the park bathroom. If we can put them at the scene by matching their hair or prints or whatever, along with your pulling them from a lineup, their gooses are cooked."

The six men in the other room still stood in the bright light, staring forward. Two of those men were now beginning to look a little nervous. A moment later, four of the men in the lineup, cops every one, stepped away from the wall and left the stage, leaving the two Latino brothers behind.

"Fuck," I heard the fat man mutter as the lights went down in their room and came up in mine. The mirror went black.

I turned to Chris and saw a smile on his face. He gave me a wink, then turned to the stenographer. "Did you get it all?"

She held up her pad and tapped the tape recorder with a fingernail. "Twice," she said, smiling. "Congratulations."

With that, she gathered up her equipment and stepped from the room.

I lifted a hand and gently touched the bandage on Chris's ear. "Is the fat guy the one who…?"

"Yeah. He's a mean bastard. They both are. We've done a good thing today, Tyler, getting them off the street."

"I don't know how to thank you," I said. "Well, actually I do, if you'll let me."

A light glinted in his one good eye. The other eye was too bunged up to show much interest. "Does that mean what I think it means?"

I surveyed his damages. "If you're up to it, yeah. It means exactly what you think it means."

"Tonight?" he asked softly.

"Tonight." I lifted his injured hand and began to bring it to my lips. Then I cast a suspicious eye on the two-way mirror.

"Don't worry," Chris said. "They can't see us."

I pulled him toward me, but to my surprise, he resisted. "We still have things to talk over, Tyler. This isn't over yet. *None* of it is over yet. You know that, don't you?"

I felt an ache swell up inside me. It was almost identical to the ache I felt after Spence had died. I studied Chris's face. His poor eye. His injured ear. He reached out and laid a hand on my arm. It was the hand without the injuries.

"There are things I have to think about, Tyler. There are decisions I have to make."

"Concerning me?"

He hesitated. "Yes."

I took in a deep breath and fought the burning sensation of tears rising to my eyes. "Do you still... want to see me?" I asked. "You said you did. Is it still true?"

His smile was sad and weary. He looked exhausted. "It will always be true," he whispered.

We let silence settle over us until we heard voices approaching out in the hall. Those voices spurred Chris to action.

"Go home now, Tyler. I'll come by later tonight. We need to talk. I have a lot to do here, so it will probably be late. That okay?"

I nodded. "No matter how long it takes. I'll wait. It's supposed to rain tonight, you know. Don't forget to wear your rubbers."

He grinned, brushed a finger down my jawline, and left the room.

AT THE house, I stood in the middle of the living-room floor and stared at the ring on my finger. I remembered Spence's eyes the night he gave the ring to me. I remembered his excitement. His sweetness. I remembered the taste of his seed on my lips after we made love. The way his sex-warmed body pressed up to mine as he helped me slip the ring on.

The memories hurt so much I pulled the wedding ring from my finger and headed straight for the bedroom to tuck it into the satin box it came in. The other slot in the box was empty. Spence's ring was still missing. For all I knew, it would always be missing.

Somehow, in my mind, the severing of the two rings tore me farther from Spence's side than even his death did. It was a division greater than material separation. It was a division of the heart. A transcendental distancing more than a physical one.

Transcendental distancing, my ass. It was bullshit. That's what it was. The distancing was all my doing. I had moved on because I had fallen in love with someone else. It was as simple as that. I was just too much of a coward to admit it. If not to Spence, at least to myself.

I snapped the satin box closed, and a burst of sadness darkened my sight. Sadness because I knew now I had truly moved on. It was Chris who filled my thoughts now. It was Chris who stirred my feelings. I closed my eyes against a rush of need and tried to figure out what I had to do.

I had to tell him, certainly. Tell him the truth. About everything. But there was more I needed to do than that. Much more.

And where was the euphoria, knowing two of Spence's attackers had been arrested? Did even that euphoria pale beneath my fear of losing Chris because of what I had done that night on the Blue Line trolley? I didn't have to ask myself that question twice. The answer was yes. Yes, a dozen times over.

It was early evening. The sky was so heavy with approaching storm clouds that dusk had morphed into night in what seemed a matter of seconds. As I sat on my deck at the back of the house and watched the rain draw nearer, waiting for Chris to arrive, I felt the hours drag over me.

There was a fear inside me that roared out its anguish every time I saw Chris's face in my mind. Every time I remembered his words. *We need to talk. There are decisions I have to make.*

I knew what those decisions were. Chris was torn between doing his job and not wanting to hurt me. The crime he had helped solve today was only the smallest part of the equation. Somehow I knew it was the trolley murder that mattered most to him. If he didn't know for sure I was the one who killed the man on the Blue Line, he certainly suspected it. The big question now was what he would ultimately decide to do with those suspicions. He had said he loved me, yes. But would even love be enough to make him turn his back on everything he believed in? Right and wrong. The law. Would he honestly be able to love someone who had broken the rules of society he believed in so strongly—the rules he worked so hard to maintain every day of his life as a cop?

Yet once in a while, that twisted little grin Chris had shot at me when I told him to wear his rubbers popped into my head, and every time it did, I drew hope from it. Maybe things weren't as dire as I thought they were. Maybe there was still a chance for a happy ending. A happy ending for Chris and me. A happy ending to all of this.

While waiting for Chris's knock at the door, I sipped a beer, too nervous to eat. Should I tell him the truth the moment he walked in? Should I confess my involvement in the trolley murder and hope he loved me enough to find a way to protect me from what I'd done? If there was concrete evidence pointing directly at me, surely I would have been arrested already, with or without Chris's involvement. The fact that I hadn't been gave me hope. A fool's hope, maybe, but hope nevertheless.

When my phone rang, I snatched it off the cradle before the second ring sounded.

His voice was hushed. I could barely hear it. "Tyler, it's me."

I pressed the phone to my ear with both hands. "Chris."

The air was filled with static for a few seconds while we each absorbed the other's presence.

"I'm glad you called," I finally said. "Are you still at work?"

"Yes. It's crazy here. A patrolman just brought in the suspect in one of my other cases, so now I'm up to my ass in paperwork. I'll be late getting there, Tyler. Maybe you'd rather I—"

"No! Please," I pleaded. "Come tonight. I need to see you. We have to talk."

"All right," he said slowly. "I'll come tonight." *Did I hear a smile in his voice? Was that what I heard? Or was I simply hearing what I wanted to hear?*

And suddenly a flurry of words spewed out of me. "There are things I need to tell you, Chris. There are confessions I need to make."

"Be quiet!" he broke in. "Don't say those things over the phone. Not even to me." His voice lowered as if he was trying not to be overheard. I could hear the clicking of keyboards in the background, the mutter of voices. He was at his desk with a dozen other desks and a dozen other detectives scattered around him. "Baby, I think I know what you want to tell me. Just don't say it now. We'll get things settled tonight. I promise. I've thought it all through. I know what we have to do."

"Do you?" I asked. "I don't think—"

"Stop," he said. "I know everything. At least I think I do. I can protect you from this, Tyler. You just have to trust me."

"All right," I said. "I trust you. I do. Just—please hurry. I need to see you. I need to be with you."

A silence fell between us. I heard the sound of soft breathing. Again I heard the bristle of his stubble scraping across the mouthpiece, and the sound of it sent a shiver of desire racing through me.

"Don't worry, baby," he whispered vehemently. "I won't let anything happen to you. I swear I won't. I love you too much to lose you now."

I swallowed hard. "I love you too," I rasped.

"Wait for me," he said in a gentle hush, and our connection was lost.

I gently hung up the phone.

It would be all right. Chris knew everything and he still loved me.

I squeezed my eyes shut to say a silent prayer of thanks. I lowered myself into my favorite chair, and still sipping occasionally at my beer, I considered the turns my life had taken in the past couple of days. I remembered Chris's proud look as he returned my ring. I thought of the fat fuck and his brother in the lineup, both cockily spouting the words I had heard the night Spence was killed. I remember the fat guy's worried expression when it finally dawned on him that his past had caught up with him. I remembered the worried, disbelieving timbre in his voice when he muttered "Fuck!" just before the lights behind the two-way mirror went out.

But most of all, I remembered Chris saying he loved me. Without hesitation. Without doubt.

That was the memory that carried me to sleep as I sat in my favorite chair while the beer bottle, forgotten, warmed in my hand.

When I awoke, the night had settled over me. The sky, clouded with approaching rain, lay dark and starless above the rooftops, shot through with occasional flashes of quickly approaching lightning that heralded the coming storm. The city sprawled expectant and tense in the darkness, waiting for it, the air heavy with the pending downpour. I could feel it in the sudden ache of my injured fingers. Maybe they weren't quite as healed as I'd thought they were.

I tried to ignore the pain, and finally I succeeded. I slept.

Hours later, a gentle sound shook me awake. It was a humming sound, tremulous and high-pitched. At first I thought it was the wind I heard. I tilted my head and listened. The night air had changed. It had a different flavor to it. I could smell the ozone of the gathering storm, the dampness on the wind that now whistled through the eaves outside. The storm was almost here.

But that sound. What was it?

Heart racing, I started up from my chair, dropping the forgotten beer bottle, then quickly snatching it off the floor before the warm beer spilled everywhere. The house was pitch-black. When I had fallen asleep, the room had still been lit by a fading evening light. Now the blackness of the moonless night, shrouded in gathering storm clouds, made the shadows in the house impenetrable.

I switched on the floor lamp beside my chair, casting a circle of light around me. I froze in place, listening for the sound again. The sound that had woken me. When it came, I recognized it for what it was—a soft plaintive moan. A whimper. I spun my head to the front door and tried to ignore the shimmer of fear that crawled across my shoulders.

The noise had come from the porch, just on the other side of my front door.

When the sound came again, I set the beer bottle aside and moved toward it.

I switched on the porch light, but nothing happened. The bulb must have burned out. I tried to peer through the window but could see nothing.

A scratching sound coming from the doorsill at my feet made me grip the doorknob and yank the door open.

A body leaped against me, knocking me off balance. I landed hard, and a second later, I heard myself laugh.

Franklin's kisses came fast and furious. He stood atop me with all four paws digging into my chest, his whole body twisting back and forth as he scraped his tongue over every inch of skin he could find, from my forehead to my chin, then back up again.

By the time I caught my breath and laughingly pushed him away, I had scrambled to my feet.

Franklin was tied to the railing with the same long leash he had been tethered to the night he disappeared.

I bent to untie the leash just as raindrops began to fall, spattering the sidewalk. A gust of rain-sodden wind lifted my hair from my forehead. I cupped Franklin's stupidly grinning face in my hands and kissed him between the eyes. He reeked of dirty dog, but I didn't care. I had never seen anything as beautiful in my life.

"You need a bath, kid. You smell like a dead goat."

A moment later, a voice spat from the darkness. "Speaking of dead goats, how's your boyfriend, faggot?"

Before I could react, a hand came out of nowhere and pushed me backward through the door. I landed flat on my back. The leash was yanked from my hand, and Franklin was kicked through the door behind me to skid across the floor on his side and collide with my hip.

My attacker stepped over the threshold behind us, and with a vicious scowl, slammed the door behind him to shut out the storm. And to close us in.

I didn't recognize the man at all. But I knew immediately who he was.

I could tell by the boots.

CHAPTER TWELVE
PAYBACK

I TRIED to scramble to my feet. But the gorilla who had shoved me through the door laughed and planted a boot against my shoulder, pushing me back to the floor. A feeble growl erupted from Franklin's throat, but the moment it did, the same boot swung around and kicked him in the ribs. With a howl of pain, Franklin cowered beneath the blow, and I wondered how much abuse he had been subjected to in the months he'd been gone.

The man looming over me shook his head in disgust. "I got me a couple of stupid mutts here, I surely do. One just as dumb as the other."

"Fuck you," I said, and he laughed. I noticed he had an incisor missing when he did. I found myself sincerely hoping that at some point in his miserable life, somebody had kicked it out of his head.

The man who stood before me was the same man Chris had chased through the Gaslamp district a couple of weeks back. He was of medium build and medium height, and his upper lip was adorned with a scraggly-ass moustache that anybody with any brains would have shaved off at the first opportunity. He had dusky skin and a shock of thick black hair, as straight as string, framing his face. He wore filthy jeans and a leather vest with no shirt beneath, displaying a decent chest with just a spattering of hair sprinkled across his reasonably flat stomach. On his feet, the motorcycle boots. Heavy and black and adorned with chains and zippers. The very same boots I remembered seeing the night Spence was killed.

The man put his hands on his knees and squatted down until we were at eye level. He studied my face like he was looking through an aquarium wall at a new and surprising form of sea life.

"Should have killed you when I had the chance," he said with a smirk. He had a cigarette tucked atop his ear like some 1950s juvenile delinquent, and he chose that moment to pop the cigarette into his mouth with a deft and surprisingly delicate movement, then pull a lighter from his pocket to light it.

"No smoking in the house," I said, and that time he *really* laughed.

"You're a cocky little fucker, aren't you?"

His hand shot out like a rattlesnake, and he slapped me across the face. Hard. When my eyeballs stopped twirling around like marbles in a bucket, I spotted Spence's wedding ring on the bastard's finger.

I saw red.

A boom of thunder caused my attacker to turn toward the window for a split second, and in that time I kicked out with my foot and cracked him a good one on the shin. Since he was still awkwardly squatting in front of me, he toppled over like a house of cards, arms and legs pinwheeling all over the place.

Unfortunately, he pulled himself up and struck out in less time than it had taken him to collapse. He straddled me with his legs, and reaching down to grab a fistful of my hair, he yanked me to my feet. As soon as I was standing, his knee shot out and buried itself in my groin. I coughed up an "Oof!" and folded over like a pocketknife, hitting the floor hard for the second time. With my nuts on fire, I squeezed myself into a fetal position, groaning and gasping for air while he stared down at me and grinned.

He hadn't even dropped his cigarette. He puffed on it as he picked up Spence's photo from the end table and studied it, enjoying his smoke and waiting for me to catch my breath and stop rolling around in agony. While he waited, he periodically tapped his ashes over me, just to be a dick.

"This is the fucker I killed," he said as if commenting on the weather, which, by the way, was now battering the outside of the house with blasts of wind and buckets of rainwater. Lightning flashes were strobing the windowpanes every few seconds, and the grumbling thunder was rolling across the heavens above our heads in a continual, clattering roar, making the California sky sound a little like a bowling alley on league night.

"Yes!" I hissed through my teeth, still clutching my crotch. "Coward!"

He tore his eyes from the snapshot long enough to gaze at me. I noticed he had a habit of sucking air through the gap in his front teeth when he was being pensive, which wasn't very often.

"I don't like queers," he said matter-of-factly, as if that should be enough to justify his act of murder on an innocent man. "Besides, what are you bitching about? You got me back."

"What the hell are you talking about?"

"My brothers," he said. "The cops are filing charges against them in the morning. So you not only got me back once, you got me back twice. They are as good as dead, just like your little Chinese boyfriend here. They'll probably never get out of prison."

"Good," I spat.

He took a long pull from his cigarette and tossed the picture across the room, where it hit the brick fireplace, splintering the glass. He nudged my ankle with his foot to get my full attention, as if he didn't have it already. "How do you think our poor mama's gonna feel about losing two of her boys? Huh?"

I was catching my breath now. The pain in my nuts had eased to a roiling ache that only periodically made me grit my teeth. "Probably not as bad as my husband's mother felt when she had to bury her dead son after you beat him to death."

He smirked and rolled his eyes. "Husband! Is that what they call it these days? Two faggots pumping each other's bungholes and gnawing each other's peckers? Jesus, what's the world coming to?"

"Murder apparently," I said, gritting my teeth once more against the pain in my groin. Again I stared at Spence's wedding ring on the bastard's finger.

He saw me looking and cast an appreciative eye on the ring. "Nice, huh? Faggots always buy the best jewelry. I'll give them that." He spit on the ring and rubbed it against the front of his vest to make it shine.

He sucked in a shot of oxygen through the gap in his teeth as if to fuel his thinking process. "I told Carlos not to pawn the other one, but the dumb shit did it anyway. That's how they caught him, you know. Him and Trini too." His eyes narrowed and oozed hate in my direction as he watched me writhe on the floor. "That and the fact that you pulled them out of a lineup."

I decided to smirk back. It was about the only form of rebellion I had available to me. "Yeah, well, if you can't do the time, don't do the crime."

"Oh, shut the fuck up," he growled, pulling a long knife from his back pocket. It looked like a fisherman's knife, with serrations on the back of the blade for scaling fish and a keen edge that caught the light and sparkled in his hand. It looked sharp as hell.

I couldn't take my eyes off it. "What are you going to do with *that*?" As he had done with the ring, he spat on the blade and rubbed it against his leg to make it shine. When he was satisfied it was as lustrous as it was ever going to be, he scraped it along his forearm to shave away a strip of hair, demonstrating for my benefit how keen the blade really was. He grinned at me all the time he did it.

Franklin scooted up close to me and rested his chin on my arm. I could feel him trembling against me. I buried my hand in the fur on his back and wished to God I was anywhere else but where I was. Since my attacker had ignored my question the first time, I decided to repeat myself.

"I said, what are you going to do with that knife?"

He smiled wide. If the missing tooth caused him any embarrassment, he certainly didn't show it. "I'm going to toss my brothers a 'Get Out Of Jail Free' card by making sure they don't have any eyewitnesses testifying against them at the trial. And seeing as how you're the only eyewitness, I guess that means carving off your fucking head. That way, see, I eliminate your big flapping mouth and your baby blue eyes all at the same time. You won't be making any accusations in that courtroom when I get done with you." He laughed. "As a matter of fact, you won't be good for much of anything, except maybe dog food." He clucked his tongue at Franklin. "What do you think of that, Dog? Want some minced faggot tongue for dinner?"

Franklin ignored the voice. I didn't. "His name isn't Dog. It's Franklin."

He nodded, as if he figured as much. "Whatever, dipshit."

He gazed around the room, then stepped away far enough to peer down the hallway leading to the rest of the house. When he was satisfied we were alone, he turned back to me.

"You look like you're doing all right for yourself. Got any other jewelry stashed anywhere? Maybe a nice pile of cash? No point chopping off your head if I can use it first to get me enough money to make this sad old life a little more bearable."

He grinned at his own sense of humor. Stalking across the room, he approached me once again and gave me a sharp kick in the leg. Just enough of a kick to get me moving. I groaned my way to my feet, and Franklin whimpered to see me move away from him. Tail down, eyes terrified, Franklin dragged himself to his feet with me and stayed close by my side, his body pressed to my leg, as if he was terrified we would be separated. He averted his eyes from the other man in the room.

I didn't have that privilege. As a matter of self-preservation, I kept my eyes on the fucker at all times.

He shepherded me toward the hallway. I had to limp to get there. My nuts were killing me.

"Show me where you hide the goodies," the goon growled.

"There aren't any goodies."

"You're lying."

I had to stall for time. Chris would be here soon. If he came directly from work, he might even be armed.

Or, I thought with a sudden burst of hope, *maybe I can arm myself.*

To do that, I needed to slow down the proceedings. Give myself time to think. And act.

"Where were you born?" I asked, grabbing at the first straw I could think of.

He stopped and stared at me. "Where the fuck do you think I was born? Right here. Mercy Hospital, if you really want to know. What the fuck is it to you?"

So the hospital that dragged me back to life after the attack was the same hospital that brought my attacker into the world in the first place. Great. Nice coincidence.

"Why do you have an accent?" I asked, as if I really wanted to know. "I figured you and your brothers were born in Mexico."

He threw his shoulders back, offended to the core. "I'm as American as you are! What'd you think I was, a wetback? If me and my brothers have an accent, it's because our parents didn't speak English. Still don't, as a matter of fact. And if you're gathering all this information to put in a book, I got news for you. You won't be alive long enough to write it. You'll be lucky if I give you time to kiss your faggoty ass good-bye."

Stall him. Stall him.

"Why did you take the dog? The night you killed Spence. Why did you take the dog?"

He grabbed a fistful of my T-shirt and dragged me toward him. His breath smelled like a putrefying whale carcass that had washed ashore on some steaming hot beach. If he had ever had a passing acquaintance with a spool of floss, it must have been in another lifetime.

"What the hell is wrong with you? Who gives a shit why I took your dog? The damn mutt is worthless anyway. I never saw him wag his tail once. Not in five months. Not once."

I couldn't stop myself. I had to smile. "I guess he didn't like the company he suddenly found himself in. He must have higher standards than I thought he did."

The man with the knife pulled me even closer. With an evil grin, he slid his rancid tongue up the side of my cheek. I almost passed out from the stench.

I jerked away. "Don't touch me like that."

His eyes narrowed into mean little slits. "Don't worry, fag. That's the only taste of me you'll ever get."

Like I cared.

Something bumped the back of my leg. It was Franklin. He whimpered softly, then emitted a soft growl. I think he was protecting me. At least that's what I told myself he was doing. I looked down at him, and a dribble of urine seeped out of him, splashing the floor.

He emitted another soft whimper and pressed himself to me. I reached down and stroked his ear.

Spence's murderer cackled. "You two deserve each other. You're both pissing your pants."

I tried to think. *How can I get to the gun in the basement? Why did I hide it so fucking far away?*

I racked my brain, trying to make time. Trying to give myself an edge. Give myself a chance. "What's your name?"

That *really* made him laugh. "What's next, asshole? Where you from? Whad'ya like to do in bed? You a top or a bottom? You queers make me sick."

"Don't hold back," I said. "Tell me how you feel. So what's your name? I always like to know my murderer's name. It's sort of a thing with me." *Stall him. Just keep stalling.*

The man who was determined to be the last human I would ever speak to simply eyeballed me up and down like he had never seen a sorrier pile of crap. "If it's that important to you, my name is Rico. Don't bother memorizing it. You won't be around long enough to use it anyway. Now where's the money stashed?"

He still held a clump of my T-shirt in his fist. He held it so tight, the collar was rubbing my skin raw at the back of my neck.

"Kitchen," I said. The last thing I was going to do was give him another crack at the wedding ring I had just had returned to me. He already had Spence's. That was bad enough. "There's some cash in the cupboard." That much was true, but my fake can of corn that was made to hide cash from the dumber segment of the burglarizing public was almost empty. I had used the money for groceries during the past months when I wasn't working. If I was lucky, good old Rico would find maybe thirty dollars in it. I had a pretty good idea that wouldn't be enough to make him happy.

Then I had a better idea. "Take me to the bank and I can draw you some cash out of the ATM. I'll give you all you want if you'll just let me go." *Maybe a trip to the bank would give me time to think. Time for Chris to get here. Time for* something!

He stomped off toward the kitchen with me in tow. Poor Franklin howled in pain when I accidentally stepped on his foot as Rico dragged me across the room. "How stupid do you think I am, faggot? Bank security cameras and all that crap? Just shut your mouth and show me what you've got in the house. And don't even think about me letting you go. That ain't gonna happen. As a matter of fact, asshole, you're already dead. You just haven't figured it out yet."

Wonderful. Just what I wanted to hear.

The storm was going gangbusters now. Flashes of lightning splintered the starless sky outside, hurling blasts of light against the windowpanes like buckets of white paint. Torrents of rainwater sluiced off the rooftop, rattling the rain gutters and splashing the windows like the house was rolling through a carwash.

Where was Chris? Where the fuck was Chris?

I made the mistake of trying to pull myself out of Rico's grip, and he whirled on me. Cramming the tip of the knife against my neck, he hissed into my ear. "Give me a reason to use it. Go ahead. It won't take much, you know. I'm ready to saw your goddamn head off right now."

I gasped against the steel tip of the knife pressing into my flesh. "Then you'll never find the money."

He laughed. "Don't kid yourself. With you out of the way, I could take my time and tear this place apart."

A brainstorm at last.

"You still won't find it," I taunted. "And even if you *do* find it, how're you going to get it open?"

He froze, the tip of his knife still pressed to my neck. I could feel a tiny rivulet of blood seeping across my Adam's apple where he had pricked my skin. *Jesus, what it is with Latinos and knives? This is the second time I've been poked in the neck by one.*

Rico relaxed the grip he had on my shirt. He pushed me out to arm's length and studied my face. "What are you saying, faggot? Are you saying you've got a safe?" He looked around the house—at my thousand-dollar TV set, the crystal dishes and Lenox china in the dining room hutch, the fox-hide throw on the back of the sofa.

"It makes sense," he said, more to himself than to me. "You've got money, don't you, faggot? You must have a really good job. What do you do, pervert? What do you do for a living?"

"I'm an accountant." That much was true, but the safe was pure fantasy. Hopefully I'd still be alive when Rico figured that out.

He stared at me for a second, then burst out laughing. "Bullshit," he said, grinning widely. "Accountants don't live this good."

I decided to slap him with a little bit of truth, just to really piss him off. "That's where you're wrong. My accounting job pays about a hundred thirty grand a year. The man you murdered in cold blood made even more money than I do. Feeling a little bit like a failure now, are you, dumbass? What did your last job pay? Five bucks an hour for flipping burgers? Twenty bucks a day for trimming hedges? Are you a yardman? Is that what you do when you're not out murdering innocent people? No," I finished up. "That's not it at all. You're just another leech on society that's never held down a job at all, right? You've never worked a day in your fucking life."

Rico's fist came out of nowhere and connected with the side of my head. I saw stars. At that precise moment, several things happened at once.

From the force of his blow, I went sliding across the kitchen floor on my back and collided with the basement door, damn near breaking my neck. My face went numb where Rico's fist had collided with it. I didn't have time to bitch about it because suddenly, and with considerable amazement, I found myself staring speechless as good old Franklin finally found his courage.

With a roar of fury, he launched himself off the floor and, sailing high, clamped his teeth into Rico's arm, dislodging the knife in Rico's hand and sending them both crashing against the kitchen table. A bowl of fruit tipped and clattered to the floor. Apples rolled in every direction.

While Rico tried to shake Franklin off and, in the process, stumbled over a kitchen chair and landed with a thud on the kitchen floor among the apples, I shook the fog from my head and clawed my way to my feet. Franklin continued to worry Rico's arm like a terrier with a rat.

Rico bellowed obscenities and rained blows on the dog, but Franklin just held on to Rico's forearm with his sharp little teeth, growling and snarling and dribbling piss everywhere. Unable to free himself from Franklin's fangs, Rico scrambled across the floor on his hands and knees, dragging Franklin along beside him, and reached out to grab the knife he had dropped. When I saw what he was doing, I kicked the knife away and wrenched open the basement door. A second later I was flinging myself down the basement stairs.

At that moment, the lights went out, and the three of us were thrown into stygian darkness.

The sudden loss of light so surprised me I lost my footing and stumbled down the remaining steps to the basement floor. In the impenetrable darkness, I shook the pain away to clear my head and get my bearings. Holy shit, it was a blackout. Lightning must have struck a transformer. I couldn't believe my luck.

"Thank you, God," I whispered through numb and bloody lips.

A roar from somewhere upstairs told me Rico and Franklin were still doing battle. I couldn't see where I was going, so I tripped my way through piles of junk on the basement floor until I crashed head-on into the furnace in the corner. I scrambled around behind it, groping in the shadows, seeking the backpack I had hidden there more than two months earlier. A spider skittered across my face, and I hardly noticed it. On a normal day, that spider would have sent me to the emergency room with a heart attack.

My scrabbling fingers finally hooked one of the straps on the backpack, and I dragged it out from behind the furnace where I could get at it. With trembling hands, I tried to work the zipper open, and at that moment, above me, I heard Franklin yelp in pain and then the sound of heavy footfalls racing down the basement steps.

"You son of a bitch!" Rico screamed, and halfway down the stairs, just as I had, he lost his footing. With a curse he came crashing to the basement floor, landing less than twenty feet from me with a horrible, thudding gasp of pain.

I frantically clawed at the backpack until I heard the zipper slide. Cramming my hand inside, I felt the cold iron of the gun and ripped it out of the bag. Feeling in the darkness for the safety, I clicked it to Off and swung around to face my attacker.

Where was Franklin? Was he still in the kitchen, or had he followed Rico down the stairs?

I slapped my thigh and immediately heard the patter of toenails crossing the basement floor toward me. When Franklin pressed his snout into my leg, I reached down, took hold of his fur to keep him next to me, and aimed the gun into the darkness ahead.

Rico's words coming out of the shadows sent chills up my spine. "You're a dead man now, faggot."

I tipped my head to the side, considering his words, then decided, *Nope. I don't think I'll let that happen.*

At the sound of a heavy boot crashing into a box of junk, the sound closer already than the voice had been, I aimed the gun into the noise and squeezed the trigger.

The flash of the gunshot strobed the room with a golden explosion of light, but the darkness returned before I could comprehend what it was I had seen. While I might not be able to see what I'd done, a wail of terror told me my shot was a good one. Something heavy hit the floor, and I heard a flurry of clattering noises that I recognized as a tool chest tipping over. A moan erupted from what sounded like the base of the stairs.

I dropped to my knees, still aiming the gun into the shadows in front of me. Franklin and I cowered against each other, each drawing strength from the other, and just as I was about to fire into the darkness again, the lights blinked back on.

RICO LAY at the foot of the stairs, his body twisted around, half-draped through the railing. My bullet had caught him in the thigh, and he was staring at the wound with wide, frightened eyes. I couldn't say I blamed him. There was a geyser of blood shooting out of the wound with such force it was sprinkling the basement floor and the stairs around him.

He pressed a trembling hand to the fountain of blood and tried to stop the flow. When he did, the blood merely seeped through his fingers, unstoppable.

"Oh, Jesus," he muttered, his face convulsed in horror. "Help me. I don't want to die."

I approached him slowly, gun in hand, unmoved by his plea. This was the bastard who beat Spence to death with an iron pipe, after all. I had no sympathy for him whatsoever.

"Spence didn't want to die either," I said calmly. And once again I was surprised to feel the calm inside me. The unshakable disconnect. My hands were steady. My heartbeat unhurried. I even felt a smile playing at the corners of my mouth as I studied the man pleading for his life at the foot of the stairs.

The warm pistol felt like a friend in my hand and I raised it to point the barrel at Rico's face. His eyes opened wider than they already were, and it pleased me to see his fear.

"Please, no," he pleaded. "Get me an ambulance. Please."

"You're bleeding out," I said, tightening my finger on the trigger. "The bullet must have snagged your femoral artery. I'll give you the option you never gave Spence. Do you want to bleed to death slowly, or do you want a bullet in the brain? Either way, it's all the same to me. The choice is yours, but you'd better choose quickly. I don't think you've got all day to piddle around about it. You're bleeding like a stuck pig."

Tears of pain and terror rolled down his cheeks. His entire leg was awash with blood. It dripped down the stairs and puddled on the basement floor. Already his face looked pale and gaunt. He pressed his hand tighter to the wound but the blood continued to flow. He licked his lips and began to weep.

"Please," he begged, "don't do this."

Franklin tensed at my side and let out a bark. At the same moment, I heard footsteps upstairs in the house. They crossed the kitchen floor, and a moment later a shadow filled the doorway at the top of the stairs. I looked up to see Chris standing there. He was soaking wet from the rain, and he held his service revolver in his left hand.

I turned away from Chris and focused my attention on Rico again. I cocked the gun, and Rico cried out in fear. I stepped closer to him, still aiming the barrel directly at his face. The sudden stench of feces told me he had soiled himself in his fear, or maybe it was from the blood loss weakening his body. Either way I could see he was appalled by what he'd done.

"You really are a coward," I said, my finger tightening on the trigger.

Chris spoke coolly from the top of the stairs. "Don't do it, Tyler. Please. Don't do it."

Rico twisted his head around to look behind him and saw the detective standing there with a gun in his hand. The gun was hanging limp at Chris's side, as if he had forgotten he still held it in his hand.

"Thank God!" Rico sobbed. "Help me. Don't let him kill me! Shoot the fucker! Shoot him!"

"Shut up," Chris said before I had a chance to, and the terror in Rico's face multiplied. He was trembling now from blood loss. His face was ashen. He barely had the strength to hold his hand over the hole in his leg to try to stem the flow of blood. And truthfully, none of his efforts so far had stemmed the flow of blood at all. It still poured through his fingers onto the steps, and from the steps, it dribbled down to the floor below. There was a pool of blood spreading out from Rico in every direction. I figured if he were a car, his oil light would be on by now.

I lifted my eyes to study Chris's face. "I have to do this for Spence," I said. "I owe him that much."

"No," Chris said gently. "Turning yourself into a murderer isn't going to change anything. Put the gun down, Tyler. We have more important things to discuss than the fate of this asshole. We need to talk about us."

Rico heard the words and sobbed. I could see the realization dawning in his eyes that there was no escaping his fate. He was going to die. There was no one willing to help him here, and even if there was, it was probably too late anyway. Even if someone called for an ambulance right then, by the time it got here, he would have bled to death. There was nothing left for him to do but die, and he knew it. Weakened and terrified, he laid his head back onto the step behind him and began to weep like a child.

I didn't move the barrel from Rico's head. My hand was as steady as stone. "I'm already a murderer, Chris. Nothing I do now is going to change that."

Chris tucked his gun in his shoulder holster and took a step down the stairs. "I know," he said softly. "You made a mistake. Grief did it, I think. Grief and a desire to strike back at the unfairness that took Spence away from you. I understand that, Tyler. I've known about the trolley murder for weeks. I recognized you on the security tape even if no one else could ID you. I recognized your movements, the way you carried yourself. I didn't turn you in, Tyler. And I'm not going to."

I couldn't drag my eyes from Rico's face. His eyes were closed now, his breath coming in weak, flurried gasps. *Was he dying? Is this what dying slowly looked like?*

"One more death won't matter, Chris. One more murder won't change me from what I already am. And what he is."

"No," Chris said, vaulting over the handrail at the side of the stairs to avoid the last remaining steps where Rico lay sprawled, bleeding out. "You've already killed him, Tyler. He'll be dead in a minute without any further help from you. But there's a way for us to fix this. A way for us to clear the slate on both murders. I don't want to lose you, Tyler. I don't want to lose you like you lost Spence. I can fix this. I can clear you of both murders."

"Why?" I asked. "Why would you do that?"

And Chris's answer came in a rush of emotion. A clap of thunder shook the house, and he raised his voice so his words would carry over the noise of the storm.

"Because I love you! I've never loved *anyone* before. Not like this. I'm not going to let you throw your life away for these animals. I'm not going to let you throw my happiness away either. I'll never be happy without you. I know I won't. Please, Tyler. If you love me like you said you do, let me fix this. Put down the gun."

"I'm sorry for what I did," Rico sobbed as he slid down the remaining steps to the basement floor and his face settled into the pool of blood still spilling from his leg. "I'm sorry."

He wasn't speaking to me. Maybe he was speaking to God. I didn't know, nor did I care. Chris and I both ignored him.

Chris approached me now, skirting the pool of blood on the floor—skirting the body lying limp in the middle of it, pleading for his life from an entity we couldn't see. "Listen to me, Tyler. Let me explain what we can do."

"No. He has to die."

"He *is* dying! Now shut up and listen."

I turned my eyes from Rico and trained them on Chris. His injured eye looked worse than it had in the afternoon. It was purple and puffed and damn near swollen shut. The bandage on his ear had come off in the rain, and I could see the stitches now where they had sewn his ear back together. One of the brothers currently in jail must have tried to rip it off his head when Chris arrested them.

But even with just one good eye, I could see Chris's love for me shining out. And his desperation too. His desperation not to let me fuck up my life—*our* lives—any more than I already had.

I lowered the gun. "Go ahead," I said. "I'm listening."

"We can let the law take care of this for us, Tyler. All we have to do is twist the facts in our favor. The man you killed on the trolley was the lowest kind of scum. He cut you with a knife. It was self-defense. Plus he was a terrible person. He deserved what he got. The man dying at your feet deserves what he's getting too. A jury would probably never convict you for killing either one of them, Tyler. But that still doesn't make it right. Let me fix this. Please."

I longed to pull Chris into my arms and weep like a child. I longed to feel his arms around me and to hear him whisper sweet things into my ear as if none of this had ever happened. But most of all, I longed to see the life spill out of the man on the floor completely.

"How?" I asked, tossing the gun aside. We both watched it skitter across the basement floor and clatter against the wall.

The only person not watching the movement of the gun was Rico. He was too weak to pay much attention to anything. His hand had slipped from the wound in his leg, and the blood now seeped from the hole unhindered. The flow had slowed. He was running out of blood to spill. Rico lay unmoving, staring at the ceiling, his eyes opened wide but seeing nothing. He reeked of feces and the metallic stench of fear. His fingers clenched spasmodically in rhythm to the flutter of his breath.

He was beyond knowing anything.

I looked back at Chris.

With my gun no longer in my hand, Chris stepped forward and pulled me into his arms. He whispered in my ear, "Let me do what I have to do."

And I nodded, weary to the bone. "All right."

"First of all, Tyler. Tell me you bought this gun illegally. Tell me it isn't registered in your name."

I tried not to look guilty when I said, "It isn't registered at all."

He nodded as if he'd figured as much. "Where did you get it?"

"I bought it from some guy on the street."

"Did you give him your name?"

"No."

"Did you pay cash?"

"Yes."

"Good. Then it can't be traced back to you."

Chris lay his hand to my cheek before gripping my shoulders and easing me aside. He stepped across the basement to retrieve the gun I had sent sliding across the floor. He checked it to make sure it was loaded, then he pulled a handkerchief from his back pocket and wiped the pistol clean of prints. Still holding it in the folds of the handkerchief, Chris knelt and pressed the gun into Rico's hand. Rico didn't seem to notice.

Lifting Rico's hand with my gun still in it, Chris aimed the gun at the wall, and covering Rico's finger with his own to apply pressure to the trigger, he shot a bullet into the wall.

"Now the residue of a gunshot will be on Rico's hand."

"I don't understand," I said. "How will that help us?"

"Twofold," Chris explained. "The gunshot residue on Rico's hand proves that Rico was a dipshit who tripped on the stairs and shot himself in the leg right after he chased you down here and put a bullet in the wall trying to kill you. But that's not all it does. When they compare the bullet used to kill the man on the trolley with the bullet the cops will think this moron pumped into himself, it will come up a match since both bullets were shot from the same gun, thus proving Rico not only shot himself like a putz, but he also killed the creep on the trolley. We already know Rico killed Spence. That's a given. Now we've not only nailed the trolley murder to his forehead but we've protected you as well." He cast an inquisitive look in my direction as if looking for a little emotional backup. "I'm assuming your career in crime has ended now. I don't want to have to be conjuring up ways to protect your ass ever again. Okay?"

I grinned. "Okay."

"And don't buy any more illegal firearms."

"I won't. Unless you piss me off."

"That was a joke, right?"

"Yes, Chris. That was a joke."

His eyes softened as he watched me. "Nothing you've done has made me stop loving you, Tyler. I want you to understand that. I know what your motives were. I know why you did what you did."

I felt tears burn the back of my eyes. "Thank you."

"Tell me you love me." Chris's voice was soft and pleading and gentle.

"You know I do," I said.

"Tell me anyway."

I sighed, but there was gratitude in it. Gratitude and a dozen other emotions. "I love you."

Franklin pranced around my legs, amused, I suppose, by the warmth in my voice. Or maybe he was just happy to be home. Who knows?

Chris looked down at him as if he had only just noticed he was there. "Are you keeping the dog?" he asked.

I reached down to pat Franklin's head. "Yes."

Chris rolled his eyes. "Waldo will be thrilled to death."

"Fuck Waldo," I said. "Tell me you love *me*."

Chris flashed his perfect teeth. I was happy to see they were all still there. Judging by the damages done to the outside of his head, I wasn't sure until I actually saw them. "I love you," he said.

Rico, at our feet, barely audible, breathed out the words. "You faggots are making me sick." Then his voice fell silent. The faint stir of his breathing stopped.

Rico was dead.

"Prick," Chris muttered, then took my hand and led me around the body and up the stairs. I ushered Franklin into the kitchen ahead of us and walked into Chris's arms.

"I have to call the cops," Chris said.

"You are the cops," I countered.

"You know what I mean."

He reached for his cell phone and punched 911. When he was finished giving directions, he dropped the phone back in his pocket and leaned against the sink, watching me.

"Don't worry," he said. "You're safe."

I handed Chris a beer from the fridge. He lifted it immediately into a toast.

"To Spence," he said.

I tapped his bottle with mine. "To Spence."

We listened to the rain and thunder until a siren drowned them out. Twenty minutes later the house was packed with people. Cops, forensic techs, EMTs. Chris and I were practically squeezed out onto the porch. Not that we minded.

We stood there watching the storm batter the city while the technicians did their work. I listened quietly as Chris explained to the investigating officer how it all went down. By the time he had finished, even I believed him. I stood silently and sipped my beer while the storm slowly retreated toward the horizon.

It was over. The saga of Spence's death. Over. The three bastards who had brought all this misery down upon our heads were now either dead or in jail. I shuddered inwardly at some of the things I had done during the course of it all, but truthfully, those actions had left almost no mark on me. I remembered them, yes, but was I sorry for what I'd done? No. As far as I was concerned, there was nothing to be sorry for. I was simply paying a debt. A debt to

Spence. And now that the debt was paid, I was satisfied I had done what I needed to do. For me. And for Spence.

As I stood on the porch, leaning against the railing, I let the cool, brisk wind from the dying storm toss my hair around. The air smelled clean and fresh, and I could almost feel it blowing away what small vestiges of guilt I might still have clinging to me, which were few if any at all. The lightning had moved off to where I could just see it sparking on the horizon. The thunder had grown silent. The storm was letting up. The rain was easing too. I could tell by the dwindling sound of raindrops, scattered now, tapping into the puddles on the sidewalk.

I patiently waited for the cops and the techs and the morgue guys to finish their jobs so I could go back into my house. Franklin stood at my feet, as patient as I was. He seemed to need my touch, my reassurance, so my fingers never left his coat. Periodically he would press his cold snout to the palm of my hand and give me a little lick as if to reassure himself I was really there.

Every few moments Chris would cast his eyes in our direction.

There was always a smile in them when he did.

CHAPTER THIRTEEN
TOUCH

CHRIS'S BREATH was warm on my face, and it smelled of mouthwash. We stood facing each other in my bedroom, just inside the sliding glass doors leading out to the deck. We had showered to wash away the long, horrific day we'd shared, and Chris was wrapped in Spence's white terry-cloth robe. I was in my blue one. The showers had come individually, not together. We hadn't quite been ready for that level of intimacy just yet.

But that was quickly changing.

His arms were around me, his hands at the small of my back, holding me close. He laid his lips softly over mine, and then slowly breaking the kiss, he turned to gaze dreamily out across the deck at the late moon shining low on the western horizon. The storm clouds had mostly passed, and the night was almost over. It had taken hours for the forensic team and other assorted cops and technicians to finish their work in the basement.

Not once had a shred of doubt or a questioning look been cast upon our story as to what had transpired there. It pays to have a homicide detective on your side when you're trying to fudge the law.

Chris brought his eyes back to me. Or I should say his *eye*. The one that was black and swollen was pretty much out of commission, and I reached up now to lay a gentle finger to it.

"Hurt?" I asked.

"Not until you touched it." He saw the surprise on my face and laughed. "Kidding, Tyler. The eye's okay. It's not the first time a perp has put his fist in my puss. Probably won't be the last time either."

"Maybe you should find a calmer line of work."

Again he surrendered a soft little laugh. "I would, but I'm afraid I'll need all my crime-fighting skills to keep you out of trouble for the rest of my life. I can't have my vigilante lover serving time in the slammer just because he feels a need to eradicate all the scumbags from the streets. It wouldn't look good on my quarterly evaluations."

I blinked at the softening look of wonder on his face. He seemed to have just realized what he'd said.

I ignored the first part of his little speech, but the second part certainly grabbed my attention. "Lovers," I said. "Is that what we'll be? Lovers?"

He touched the side of my neck with his fingertips as if to gauge my heat. "Until you're ready to wear that wedding ring again. Sure. If you'll have me. I'm crazy about you, Tyler. I have been since the first day I saw you. I'm not going to let you out of my sight now. I've worked too hard to stake my claim. You're mine forever."

"I'm pretty high maintenance." I grinned.

"No shit."

I let my gaze burrow into his. As always, when he looked at me, he was an open book, offering everything of himself and hiding nothing from me. That was one of the things I loved about him. "Did you ever think this was wrong, Chris? Our coming together? You know, with your being the cop in charge of my case. Did it ever cross your mind that perhaps we were stepping over the line? Going where we really shouldn't be going at all?"

He offered up a tiny shrug. "The thought occurred to me. But every time I looked at you, I pushed those niggling doubts away. I had to. Right here, Tyler, right now—standing where we are with our arms around each other—this is where I've always known we would end up. In my head it was a done deal the first moment I laid eyes on you. Of course, I didn't know you were going to start killing people left and right like a fucking Hun. That sort of put a crimp in our burgeoning relationship."

"Blow me," I said, smiling.

"Don't rush me," he said. "I'll get to that."

It was my turn to laugh, but Chris obviously hadn't finished what he wanted to say. He waited until I stopped giggling before he picked up his train of thought and carried it a little farther down the tracks. "The more important question, I think, is does it feel wrong to *you*?" he asked. "Our being here like this?"

I leaned forward to press my forehead to his. His skin was hot against mine. "No, Chris. It feels exactly right."

"Good."

It was my turn to stare out at the emerging stars as they peeked one by one from beneath the vanishing storm clouds. It was almost as if they were being rolled out for my viewing pleasure. The air smelled crisp and clean and cool from the rain. From somewhere the scent of honeysuckle drifted through the window.

The words I had just spoken were not quite true, and I knew it. Chris seemed to know it too.

He took my chin in his hand and pivoted my head toward him. "You're thinking of Spence. You're thinking it's too soon to move on. Things aren't exactly right after all, are they?"

"N-no. Not really. It's only five months. What's an acceptable time frame for letting an old love go and taking a new love in? I just can't help but wonder how Spence would feel about it. How Spence would feel about *us*."

Chris answered me in that gentle, mellow baritone that always stirred me so when I heard it. It somehow gave me the impression he had pondered his words for hours before actually deigning to utter them. No lie could ever be carried on a voice such as that. And in truth, I don't believe Chris ever had a lie inside him to speak. Not when it came to his feelings. "He loved you, Tyler. He would want you to be happy."

I watched Chris's lips as he spoke. They were so beautiful. And his teeth behind them, so white and small and perfect. "I know. I know he would."

My heart quickened as Chris slid a hand inside the lapel of my robe to rest it on my bare shoulder. He leaned in to me and whispered in my ear, "I've wanted this for so long."

"Me too," I breathed, absorbing the heat of his fingers on my skin. I could feel my cock expanding, growing hard. That "blow me" remark earlier had started the blood flowing. It surely had. And most of it was flowing south.

But Chris wasn't quite ready to go there yet. He obviously still had things on his mind.

"You were lucky, you know. Lucky your face couldn't be seen on that surveillance tape at the trolley station. Lucky nobody saw you on the train. Lucky you didn't leave a fingerprint anywhere."

I was still forced to close my eyes and thank God every time I thought about how my crime spree *might* have ended. "I know, Chris. I think about it a hundred times a day."

He studied my face in the moonlight. "And still no regrets?"

"Maybe a few," I admitted. "But I still think Spence deserved a little vengeance. I'm not sorry I gave it to him. As far as I'm concerned, I simply did what I had to do."

"Yes, but by doing it you risked your own life and freedom. You know that, don't you? You also risked my happiness."

"Your happiness?"

"Yes."

I lost myself in the honey of his eyes as he watched me, waiting for my response. "Thank you for saying that," I said. "I really do love you, you know. And for the first time in months, I feel safe with you here." I tapped my chest. "I mean *here*, Chris. Here in my heart."

I rested my hand on the back of his neck, carefully so as not to bump his injured ear. My other hand I laid on his arm. I felt a rush of desire sweep through me at the bristly, masculine feel of the muscle and hair beneath my caress. He lifted his hand from my shoulder and slid it downward across my chest. I felt my knees begin to shake as he pressed his palm to the spot on my chest that was just atop my heart, as if he wanted to feel the beat of it in his hand. When he did, his fingertip came to rest directly over my tracheotomy scar. He stroked it gently, then bent his head and leaned in to press his lips to the scar.

"Thank you for letting me in," he whispered, his mouth still pressed to the base of my throat. "I'll try to make you happy."

I had to swallow before I could form the words. "So will I."

I was fully hard now. And so was he. I could feel our cocks tenting the robes we were wearing, but still we made no sexual move toward each other.

Chris pulled back to smile at me and his good eye crinkled merrily. His other eye was too puffed up to move. "Judging by his pictures, Spence was one of the most handsome men ever," he said. "I hope you don't mind lowering your standards now that you're stuck with me."

Did he honestly not know how he looked? "Chris," I said, "every time I lay eyes on you, you take my breath away. Don't you know that?"

His face darkened in the dim light. I was pretty sure he was blushing. "Really?"

"Really."

He clumsily cleared his throat, and his hand on my chest brushed my nipple, causing me to shudder. When he felt the tremor go through me, he gently took my nipple between his thumb and forefinger. He didn't tweak it, he didn't squeeze, he simply held it there. I found myself having to remember to take a breath.

I enjoyed the sensation for five or six seconds, then opened my eyes to stare at him. "I haven't had sex for five months," I said.

He smiled. "Unless you count my jacking off thinking about you, I'm pretty sure I have you beat."

"You jacked off thinking about me?"

"Don't ask."

"That's funny," I said, smirking. "So did I. Thinking of you."

He smirked back. "That's a lie."

"No, it isn't," I said.

He studied my face. "No, I guess it isn't."

I felt myself smile. "Well, this shouldn't take long then. Sex, I mean."

"Nope." He grinned. "Not long at all."

"Just so you know," I said. "I'm out of shape. I haven't been exercising."

"Neither have I."

"Yeah, but you've been chasing crooks. That's sort of like jogging."

He gingerly touched his mangled ear. "Well, not exactly."

"I'm pale too," I added. "I haven't been out in the sun since this whole thing happened."

"I don't care, Tyler. I like pale men."

"Oh, please," I groaned, and he laughed.

And suddenly our minds seemed to have turned the corner. We stood tense in each other's arms, and I wondered who would make the first move.

He released my nipple and slipped his hand beneath my arm to caress my side. I almost gasped at the tender stroke of his long fingers on my rib cage.

"What do you like?" he asked softly.

"Movies, long walks, Toyotas."

He barked out a laugh. "You know what I mean. Sex, Tyler. I'm talking about sex."

"I like it all," I said, no longer joking. "I like you. I want to please you. Whatever you want, that's what I want."

His other hand slid inside my robe to brush my other side. With his movement, I felt the belt on my robe loosen.

I remembered his injuries. "I don't want to hurt you."

"Then don't break my heart."

"I mean your *physical* injuries."

"Oh. Well, if you make me cry, I'll try not to let you know. Just don't stick anything in my ear. That hurts like a motherfucker."

"I'll try to remember." We both dissolved in giggles, but they died quickly enough when I slipped my hands into Chris's robe and gripped his naked waist, just as he had done to me. His body was satin heat beneath my fingers, unfamiliar and new. I just stood there, my breath stilled, loving the way he felt.

His mouth found mine and I pulled him close. When I did, I felt his cock press into me.

"Oh, sweet Jesus," he murmured low, and a moment later, he pushed my robe from my shoulders, and I felt it slide off my back and fall crumpled at my feet.

I stood naked and hard before him.

He shrugged out of his own robe, and the next thing I knew, we were together. Naked. For the very first time.

His body felt like heaven against mine. I slid my hands down his back until I met the slope of his butt. His ass was firm and lean and brushed with a fine sprinkling of hair. I dipped a finger between his cheeks and tugged him closer. He buried his face in the crook of my neck as his hard cock lay like heavy fire against my stomach.

I pushed him gently away, just far enough for me to see him. He looked exactly as I had imagined he would. His torso was almost hairless but for a small patch of dark hair nestled in the center of his chest. Another trail of bristle trailed down from his navel to the pillow of pubic hair cradling his cock. His legs were long and lean and coated with hair. His shoulders were broad. His dick was circumcised, the corona fat and pink, the erect shaft roped with veins. There was a gleam of moisture shimmering on the tip of it. I dropped to my knees in front of him and pressed my face alongside the heavy shaft of flesh. He gasped as I kissed his stomach. Then I couldn't wait another moment, and I slid my tongue along the length of his cock until the head of it lay hot and firm against my lips. Trembling with desire now, I licked the glimmer of precome away, and the moment I tasted him on my tongue, I felt his legs buckle against me.

I started to pull him into my mouth completely, but he gripped me beneath my arms and pulled me to my feet, severing the connection. But only for a moment.

He twisted my body around until the backs of my legs were against the bed, and when he had me where he wanted me, he lowered me gently down. I butt-crawled up the bed as he stared down at me, watching. When my head was on my pillow and I was laid out naked before him, he gave a tiny sigh and lowered himself onto the bed beside me.

He laid his mouth to mine, and I tasted his tongue as he slid it through my lips. He rose up onto his knees beside me on the bed and gazed at me in the moonlight. He softly stroked the down on my legs, his forearm brushing my cock when he did. He smiled when he felt me tense. Throwing one leg over both of mine, he squatted above me, once again pressing our hard cocks together. His strong knees cinched my hips. He bent to taste my mouth again, and when he did, I felt his hands splay themselves over my stomach, kneading my flesh.

His words were almost lost in a ragged expulsion of air. "You feel incredible."

I couldn't speak. I simply lay my hands to either side of his face.

"Ow," he said, when my fingertips brushed the stitches in his ear.

"Sorry," I muttered, but he only smiled.

He kissed my chest, then let his mouth wander down across my stomach until his chin bumped my dick. And there, with a wondrous smile spreading his lips wide, he lifted my cock in his hand and held it firm and upright as he explored the head of it with his tongue.

I gasped and trembled as my ass came off the bed at the attentions of his mouth.

And then, with one hand reaching down to cup my balls, he slipped my dick between his lips for the very first time. I threw my head back, devouring the sensation. When I looked down to see him tasting me, my cock buried deep in his mouth, his eyes opened wide, and he stared right back at me, unashamed.

"Turn around," I managed to mutter, and without removing my cock from between his lips, he twisted his body across the bed until he was pointed in the opposite direction.

Easing myself over onto my side without pulling away from his mouth, I buried my face in his crotch, inhaling the clean scent of him, relishing the feel of his taut balls against my chin, his stiff, heavy cock pressed hard against my lips. When I opened my mouth to take him in, just as he had done to me, I thought, *Yes, this is right. This is exactly right.*

Later, when he came, I came at the very same moment. We lay in a trembling embrace, holding each other tight as we emptied ourselves into each other, our bodies damp with sweat, our skin alive and dancing with every sensation imaginable.

We continued to make love until the morning sun peeked over the horizon, warming us on the bed. When we finally began to doze, sated, Chris muttered into my ear before sleep overtook him.

"Forever," he said. "Forever, Tyler. Remember."

I nodded into the crook of his neck. "Forever," I whispered back. And we each drifted off in the other's arms, smiling. Our faces close. Our bodies closer.

We would stay that way until Franklin came scratching at the bedroom door, begging for his breakfast.